"The Nephilim were in the earth in those days, and also after that, when the sons of God came in unto the daughters of men, and they bore children to them; the same were the mighty men that were of old, the men of renown."

Genesis 6:4

"And the angels who did not keep their positions of authority but abandoned their own home – these he has kept in darkness, bound with everlasting chains for judgment on the great Day."

Jude 1:6

ONE DAY IN
NEW YORK

AN ARKANE THRILLER
J.F. PENN

One Day in New York. An ARKANE Thriller Book 7
Copyright © J.F. Penn (2015). All rights reserved.

www.JFPenn.com

ISBN-13; 978-1508643579

ISBN-10: 1508643571

Requests to publish work from this book should be sent to:
Joanna@TheCreativePenn.com

Cover Design: Derek Murphy, Creativindie Book Covers
Interior Design: JD Smith Design

CHAPTER 1

FOR ALL THE HYPERVIGILANCE of New Yorkers at the slightest possibility of terrorism, they embrace anything that could be construed as modern art. That's why no one reported the man constructing a strong wooden cross on the High Line that afternoon, next to a section that over-looked the Hudson River to the west. He was young and good looking with an easy smile, his Mediterranean skin burnished by the late sun. He caught the attention of female joggers as they ran past, noting his strong, muscular arms as he sawed the wooden planks. There was a handwritten sign on a cardboard rectangle propped up near his work-bench: *Performance art in progress.* That was all the passers-by needed to know, answering any questions that came to mind about his actions.

Later that day, as workers began to stream out of the local offices on the commute home, an older man stopped for a moment. He looked down at the rough wood as the man fixed the cross piece, banging in long nails to hold the planks together.

"You've got that wrong, you know," the man said. "All evidence suggests that the cross Christ died upon would have been more like a T-shape."

The carpenter paused a moment.

"The emphasis of this particular piece is more about emotional resonance than historical truth." He had a slight French accent, but in this city of diversity, that was not markedly unusual. The older man nodded slowly, rubbing his fingers across his beard before he moved on, just another walker enjoying the evening sun.

The High Line was a disused railway track, raised above the streets of Lower West Side Manhattan and transformed into a boulevard of wild grasses, flowerbeds and wooden seating where bees buzzed and birds sang in the heart of the city. The views out across the city landscape and the wide river made it a tourist draw as well as a haunt for local runners and walkers, desperate for a moment of peace above the throng. There were places on the High Line where nature had reclaimed a little corner of the metropolis, and those who craved escape came here to temporarily relieve the itch of the city. Buskers played along these sections, the sound of a jazz saxophone easing the evening into night, and still the carpenter worked on, building a base to hold the cross steady when he raised it into the sky. When that was done, he fixed pieces of rubber tire onto the cross at jaunty angles, the black material lending an urban grittiness to the simple wooden frame, a dark foil for the sunset.

As the night grew darker and the bars began to fill up below the High Line, street food vendors set up stalls to cater to those who wanted dinner with their nature walk. Far more convenient than the wilderness any day and just a stroll from Midtown. The carpenter bought a taco and watched people as they passed. His sign on the ground had gathered a few dollars over the day, perhaps a manifestation of guilt from the city elite for the artlessness of their own lives, briefly assuaged by paying another to be creative on their behalf – like doubting believers paying tithes on a Sunday. Several people had taken photos as he worked, and later those pictures would find their way into the papers. But the carpenter had no fear of discovery, for soon he would be heading back to the monastery – beyond the reach of the tentacles of this sinful city. He understood the necessity of what was to come, but he longed for peace and solitude.

He looked at his watch. Only one more part of the structure remained to be built, a simple pulley mechanism that would help lift its weight so the cross could be drawn upright and seen from the city streets below. The carpenter turned back to his work, clearing his mind of the sounds of the sinners around him. When the relic was recovered, they would be screaming soon enough.

After the final nail was hammered in, the carpenter sat in the dark, waiting, his breathing a calm meditation. As the clock neared two a.m., this area of the city was quieter. Most of the bars were closed but, of course, New York is the city that never sleeps. An audience could be guaranteed for their spectacle at any time.

He heard a car pull up on the street below, the bang of a door and the sound of several pairs of footsteps followed by a dragging sound and the shuffling of feet. The carpenter remained still, every sense heightened. Then a whistle came from the dark in the agreed pattern. He relaxed. The time had come, and now they would need to move fast.

The carpenter pulled a large holdall from beneath the bench he sat on. Unzipping it, he lifted out several cans of gasoline and began to douse the base of the cross. He poured the liquid up around the cross piece, making sure the fragments of tire were coated. The stink of the accelerant made him cough, and he tried to stifle the noise.

Two men ascended from the nearest staircase, half dragging a figure between them wrapped in a voluminous cloak. All three had their heads covered. As they came closer, the men pulled back their cowls. The carpenter looked away from the taller figure, his once handsome face disfigured by rubbled and lumpy skin, dark in places where the pigment had changed. There were rumors of an assassination attempt, a power play gone wrong. Many had tried to kill this man, and all had failed. He wasn't a Confessor, but the carpenter had heard of his relationship with the upper echelons, and knew his orders must be obeyed. The other man was the Monseigneur, the most senior Confessor in New York, with closely cropped white hair and wrinkled skin, but eyes that were as hard as the stone he knelt to pray on. The carpenter crossed himself, bowing towards his superior.

The two men dragged the captive forward. The figure tripped and fell sideways, staggering a little. The cowl slid off and the carpenter stifled a gasp. He hadn't expected a woman, even as he knew the servants of evil came in all forms. The woman's head drooped on her chest, her long grey hair loose about her face. She had been badly beaten, and blood stained the clothes he could see beneath the folds of the cloak. Her face was swollen and mashed, and a stained gag was wrapped around her mouth. She opened her eyes as the stink of gasoline roused her, and the carpenter was hypnotized by the piercing blue. He crossed himself again as the two men dragged the woman to the cross.

"I hope you've prepared well," the Monseigneur grunted. "She would only speak of the ivory artifact. The location of the corpus is still unknown, but it's a step in the quest. For now, she will be a sign to those who know how to look."

He pushed the woman down. She tried to crawl a little way and the Monseigneur grabbed her by the hair and pulled her back to the cross, forcing her to lie upon it.

They used rope to tie her wrists to the cross piece and her feet to the shaft. The carpenter doused a long strip of linen with more gasoline and then wound it around her waist and torso, further binding her to the wood. She didn't make a sound as they worked, and the carpenter avoided her gaze, crossing himself repeatedly. This was for the glory of God, wasn't it? He had been told that this action would help the

J.F. PENN

Confessors with the mission to this city, for if something wasn't done, the fate of Sodom and Gomorrah would take down this island of iniquity. But he hadn't expected that the sign to the world would be this old woman.

A siren came from the road below. The men froze in their work, waiting for it to pass before they continued. When the woman was finally well attached, they hoisted the cross up so she hung there, silhouetted against the backdrop of the city lights.

"God spoke to Moses through a pillar of fire," the Monseigneur said. "Tonight he will speak through this sacrifice."

The scarred man held up a smart phone and activated a camera, focusing it on the crucifix. The carpenter pulled a lighter from his bag along with several tapers. The men each took one and the Monseigneur began to pray aloud in Latin, his voice unwavering. They lit the ends, their faces illuminated by the flaring light. The woman finally seemed to realize what was happening and she began to thrash on the cross, the bonds loosening a little at her wrists as she moaned against the gag.

The Monseigneur leaned forward with his taper, touching the flame to the accelerant on the base of the cross, and the scarred man stretched up to apply his to the end of the cloth wrapped around the woman's torso. His smile spoke of dark desires and the carpenter crossed himself again as he touched his own taper to the base of the cross. He averted his eyes from the woman, who twisted as the flames caught the folds of her gown and billowed around her thin legs. The smell of cooking flesh weaved through the air, mingling with the gasoline. The first of the tires caught and black smoke billowed into the sky.

"Beautiful," the scarred man said with a sigh, zooming his camera in on the woman's tortured face. The whoop of sirens cut through the crackling of flames. "It's a shame we can't stay until the end."

The three men walked away from the burning cross, but the carpenter turned back as they reached the stairs. For a moment, he thought he could hear the beat of huge wings fanning the flames into brightness, but there was nothing behind the sacrifice. The woman writhed in her bonds, her hair on fire, scarlet orange against the black smoke – like the spirit of the elements alighting upon her. She was a human torch with the pitch of Hell and the flames of Satan. The carpenter could hear her screams behind the gag and he hoped that she would succumb to the smoke before the fire consumed her flesh. He crossed himself one last time and followed the others down to the streets below.

CHAPTER 2

HISSING FILLED HIS CONSCIOUSNESS, the head of the viper bobbing and weaving as it reared to strike. He tried to back away but he was cornered in the tunnel, the rock trapping him. The snake darted forward and sharp pain blossomed on his skin, setting his blood aflame as he felt the fangs sink into his flesh.

Jake Timber woke with a start, heart racing, sweat on his skin, breath coming hard. He ripped the eye mask from his face with a gasp.

"Are you alright, sir?" An air stewardess leaned over him.

Jake shook his head, clearing the vision of the nightmare. "Yes … I'm fine, thank you."

"Then would you please fasten your seatbelt?"

She smiled and walked on to attend to other passengers as the announcement came over the tannoy.

"Cabin crew, prepare for landing."

Jake looked out of the window as the plane descended through the clouds. He craved coffee, but it would have to wait now. He couldn't seem to get enough rest at the moment, and he knew his body still suffered the residual poison from the snake bite he'd suffered in Israel on the last mission. He rubbed at his arm; the puncture marks had faded, but the memory still lingered. The nest of snakes deep in the caves of Sodom appeared in his nightmares now, mingling with his memories of Africa.

His ARKANE partner, Morgan Sierra, was still in Israel, sitting shiva in mourning for a friend who had been lost in their last battle. Jake pushed down the guilt he felt for leaving Morgan alone, for not being the partner she needed. Instead, he had been medically evacuated from Israel as she pursued the Key to the Gates of Hell on her own. But mourning was something she needed to do alone, and Jake had welcomed the chance to come to New York on what was supposed to be a quick mission – a favor for the local office, which was busy at the best of times. He needed the distraction.

Jake pulled the smart phone from his bag and scrolled through the files that Martin Klein had sent. There was a special exhibition later today at the Cloisters, part of the Metropolitan Museum of Art in northern Manhattan. The central item on display was a cross of curious origin and unique carvings, hidden for generations but now on show. The Cloisters Cross, as it was known, had come up in some chatter ARKANE had detected in an extremist forum they monitored on the dark net. The Arcane Religious Knowledge And Numinous Experience Institute was a secret research center for investigating supernatural mysteries across all religions, but recently it was the rise of Christian fundamentalism that had raised red flags. This cross was supposedly connected to a relic, rumored to be the blood of a dark angel, and it had attracted the attention of a number of fringe groups.

The museum of medieval artifacts was not considered a high-risk location, but the New York office had requested a European agent on the ground, someone who could blend into the medieval academic milieu. Jake had happily volunteered, needing something to keep his mind off Morgan, although he was usually more at home in leather than tweed.

If he was honest, this was also about testing himself

and getting his confidence back again. A string of injuries had plagued Jake's last few missions, and he found himself questioning his ability in the field. He was even considering whether he should stay with ARKANE; whether Morgan would be better with another partner. He hoped this time away would help him with that decision.

Walking out of the security area a little later, Jake scanned the rows of people for a sign with his name on it. A little boy rushed from behind the barrier, his arms raised high.

"Daddy!" he shouted, leaping into the arms of a man nearby who bent to embrace his son. Jake couldn't help but smile, despite the pang that clenched his heart. Airports were always emotional places for those without family.

He was supposed to be met by one of the local agents, but he didn't know who it was going to be. Jake knew few of them by name, as he'd been focused mainly on Europe and Africa so far in his career. This would be his first time working with ARKANE stateside. Although London was the main ARKANE office, New York was a big local hub for the investigation of religious and supernatural mysteries in North America. The public face of ARKANE was academic, a research institute for religious objects, but the reality was more complicated – a battle waged daily between the forces of good and evil that most would consider myth. There were certainly enough cases here to keep the team occupied.

As Jake scanned the crowd, he caught sight of a stunning mixed-race woman, her black hair long and shiny, her dark skin almost luminous. She smiled at him and he couldn't help but return the greeting. He was surprised when she held his eyes, waving as she weaved between the crowds of people and approached him. She wore a navy blue tailored suit that suggested she worked in the halls of bureaucracy, but still managed to flatter her curves.

"I'm Naomi Locasto," she said, holding out a slim hand. "I'm with the ARKANE team here in New York, and I'll be working with you today."

Jake took her hand, shaking it as he tried to stop himself staring. Her unusual features gave her the look of a super-model, her full lips African American, her dark eyes and arched eyebrows almost Latino and her straight black hair a shade of Native American. *Welcome to New York*, Jake thought. Perhaps this trip would be more than just a distraction.

"We've had a crazy morning already," Naomi said, as she led Jake towards the pickup area. "A woman was crucified and burned to death on the High Line before dawn. No one has claimed it yet, but the police notified us because of the religious overtones of the murder."

"Who was the victim?" Jake asked as he climbed into the passenger side of the car.

Naomi frowned. "We can't seem to trace her. The body was burned beyond recognition. There's nothing at the scene to identify her and no matching missing persons record. All we know is that she was an older woman who hadn't given birth, and that she died horribly. To be honest, we thought about canceling our attendance at the Cloisters exhibition today, but since you're here …"

"I'm happy to go alone," Jake said. "It's just a monitoring exercise as I understand it, and it's a good chance to brush up on my medieval history."

"You don't really look like an academic," Naomi said, glancing sideways as she pulled out into the freeway traffic headed towards Manhattan. Jake could see she noticed his corkscrew scar, just one of the many that knitted his body together. "Can I ask where you're from? Your accent has a hint of something not quite British."

"I'm from South Africa," Jake said. "But I've lived and

worked in England a long time now. Archbishop Desmond Tutu once called my country the Rainbow People of God, but these days it's more of a shattered prism. There are engrained attitudes on so many sides that I struggle to be there ... plus, there's no one left to go back for anymore." Jake stared out of the window, surprised to be sharing such intimate details about his homeland with a complete stranger. But something about this woman set him at ease. He looked back at her. "Besides, I prefer a culture of blended people, those whose history has allowed for more intermingling over time, and London gives me that."

Naomi smiled.

"That's why I love New York too," she said. "In this melting pot of cultures, relationships naturally happen between people of all walks of life, like my own blended family. My maternal grandparents are Eastern European Jewish and African American, and on my father's side I have Cherokee and Puerto Rican blood." She smiled with pride. "I rise above definable race categories but in this town, that makes me pretty normal. I love that."

"I think you'd like London, too."

Naomi glanced over, her dark eyes holding a hint of flirtation. "Maybe I'll come visit sometime."

A beat of silence and Jake turned to gaze out the window again as they headed into town. There was a strange sense of the familiar as they drove through the city. New York was one big movie set, where the fire hydrants and yellow taxis immediately made the visitor feel at home, as they had been seen so many times before on screen. The street signs, the accents, the architecture – it was all familiar and oddly comforting.

Jake watched a pedestrian traffic sign shift to WALK and a wave of suits crossed the road, eyes fixed forward in big-city anonymity. *Don't look at me and I won't look at you.* As in London, you could be anyone in New York, and no one would bat an eyelash. The dwellers of this urban jungle were protective of the unusual and extreme, the right to stand out as sacred as that of making cold hard cash.

Naomi looked at her watch as they drove onto Manhattan Island.

"We'll go straight to the museum," she said. "We don't want to miss the tour before the grand unveiling of the cross."

Fifteen minutes later, they pulled into the driveway leading up to the Cloisters museum and gardens. The complex was part of the Metropolitan Museum of Art, but the Central Park location meant that the latter was always packed and busy. In comparison, this was an oasis of calm at Fort Tryon Park in the very north of Manhattan, a collection of medieval art in a rebuilt monastery overlooking the Hudson River. It was a surprising slice of European heritage in the modern city.

The architects had managed a coherence in the structure even though the buildings were made up of several different cloisters, rectangular courtyards for prayer and contemplation. The strong Romanesque style of the eleventh and twelfth centuries was characterized by round arches and barrel vaults, while the Gothic made itself known through pointed arches and freer ornamentation. It was a kind of architectural Frankenstein, constructed out of bits of history from French and Spanish monasteries, the effect one of unusual style elements blended by a passion for the medieval world.

The bright sun cut through Jake's fatigue and he closed his eyes for a second, letting it warm his face as they pulled into the carpark. In these little moments of calm, it was good to just be grateful for a warm day.

"Stay there a moment," Naomi said, getting out of the car. Jake opened his eyes to see her walking towards a silver van selling coffee. He smiled. Some of the places he traveled for ARKANE made it hard to get a good brew, but at least here in New York, it was pretty much guaranteed. Naomi returned with two steaming cups and a couple of pastries in a bag.

"You're a lifesaver," Jake said. He took a bite of the crumbling sweetness and sipped his coffee, starting to feel more human again. "So tell me why you're babysitting me for this little trip?"

"I'm a linguist," Naomi said, her dark eyes fixed on Jake. "There are over 800 languages spoken in New York, and many of the religious and supernatural occurrences require language expertise. Of course, I don't speak them all, but I love a challenge so I tend to get assigned to most cases in one way or another. The cross we're here to see has an unknown script on it that can't be translated. Some say it's a form of corrupted Hebrew, a mistake from the Middle Ages, but I want to see it for myself. To be honest, I'm not usually in the field – I'm office bound, but none of the other agents were up for this assignment."

"The notes I was sent imply the cross was originally British. Is that right?" Jake said. He took a bite of the second pastry.

Naomi nodded. "The provenance has never been proved, and the British government didn't buy it originally because the art dealer wouldn't reveal his source. But one scholar suggests it was originally from the Abbey of Bury St Edmunds, one of the wealthiest monasteries in England."

"Until Henry VIII dissolved them all, of course," Jake said, wiping the crumbs on a napkin. "Let's go see this marvel."

CHAPTER 3

JAKE AND NAOMI WALKED into the Cloisters main entrance, and an usher directed them towards a small group of specially invited scholars milling about as they waited for the tour prior to the unveiling of the cross. There was a muted excitement in the air, a level appropriate for academics whose passion remained of the more intellectual kind. The group congregated in one of the main Cloisters, a rectangular court constructed from fragments of the Benedictine monastery of San Miguel de Cuixà near the Pyrenees. Columns of Languedoc marble in shades of coral surrounded a garden with a fountain in the center, the sound of the water a peaceful refrain. Jake had a peculiar sense of being transplanted in time and space, the European architecture making it seem as if he had flown across the ocean for hours, only to arrive in nearby France.

A man stepped up into one of the Gothic arches so he was framed by the dark stone. He brushed his thinning grey hair to one side, pushed his glasses up his nose and coughed slightly to get the attention of the group. He waited for a hush before starting, his voice reedy and slightly high pitched with nerves.

"Welcome, esteemed colleagues from around the world. I'm the curator of artifacts and today we're so excited to share the Cloisters Cross with you, revealed for the first time in its entirety. Well, almost." The curator smiled. "We have hunted down the base of the artifact but the figure of Christ, the corpus, continues to evade us. Still, it is truly a marvel to see this impeccable and unique medieval artifact. It is one of only three almost complete medieval crosses in the world." He paused for dramatic effect. "Follow me."

The curator turned and walked through the archway, followed by the group of academics – mostly men and a few older women. Naomi certainly stood out in the crowd and Jake noticed a few appreciative glances in her direction.

It was cool as they walked through the stone corridors, surrounded by the glories of medieval Europe. One door was flanked by a pair of sculpted figures that guarded the entryway, while around them on the walls was a bestiary of animals. Jake found his pace slowing as he looked from side to side, noticing a dragon curling its tail around a tree portrayed in sepia fresco.

"It's an amazing place," he whispered to Naomi. "It feels so familiar and yet, the way it's arranged jars somehow, like something is just out of place."

Naomi shook her head with a smile. "I know, and I can't believe I haven't visited before. Living in New York for so long and yet I still don't know all its treasures."

They emerged into another courtyard open to the sky above. The curator paused. The scent of lavender and rosemary filled the air, overlaying a more complex aroma.

"We have a medieval garden here at the Cloisters," he said. "We grow the herbs, fruits and flowers that the monks would have had in those far-off times. Tending of the gardens was considered a holy duty, as much as prayer, and we like to think we continue to praise the Creator with our efforts. In celebration, we would like to offer you all some tea made from our garden of medieval herbs before we proceed into the main event."

The curator waved a hand and a group of servers carried trays forward, handing out steaming cups of hot liquid, the smell an enticing mixture of flower petals and a medicinal tinge of peppermint.

Jake handed a cup to Naomi and took one for himself, blowing on it a little before taking a sip. There was an aniseed note, a floral edge, and the overall taste was refreshing – perfect for jet lag. Around them, the academics drank enthusiastically, discussing the vintage as if it were a rare wine. Then they followed the curator onwards into a large room, with stone blockwork like the walls of a castle turret. It had a low ceiling held up by arched spines and columns topped by carvings of plants. Windows on one side let in a blueish light from outside. In the center of the room, a cross stood mounted on a stone plinth, starkly illuminated from above to highlight the elaborate carvings. It was delicate, slightly bowed in shape, and a warm golden color. A hush fell over the group as they gathered around the sacred object.

The curator held his hands together, fingertips touching as if he was about to pray. His voice was sonorous, the acoustics resonating his words as he spoke with gravitas.

"It has been said that the symbolism on the Cloisters Cross is akin to that of the Sistine Chapel compressed into an object you can hold in your hands. It's made of morse ivory, the traditional term for walrus tusk, carbon dated to the end of the seventh century. It was perhaps 500 years old when it was carved, so it was already an object of antiquity."

The curator walked around the cross, reveling in his chance to impress a captive audience with his knowledge. "You need to examine it from all angles to appreciate the master craftsmanship as the carvings emerge from all surfaces. It was originally decorated with color, and traces of ultramarine blue, malachite and vermilion have been found on the surface, all pigments used by Romanesque artists." The curator tilted his head to one side, gazing at the cross.

"Personally, I prefer the unadorned simplicity. Come, you may gather closer to examine it."

The center of the cross was a round engraved medallion. Each of the top three arms ended in a square terminal, where other tiny carvings could be seen. The long shaft of the cross held the pattern of a pruned tree trunk. Jake bent to look more closely at two tiny figures, Adam and Eve, clinging to the bottom of the Tree of Life, their faces upturned to Heaven in desperation. Moses was portrayed with the Brazen Serpent lifted high on a forked stick, and each individual figure on the cross had a different face, turned to show an aspect of their biblical character. It was truly a masterpiece.

As they stepped closer to examine it, Naomi stumbled a little, and Jake reached out to help her. She frowned and looked at the ground, confusion in her eyes.

"Are you okay?" Jake whispered, taking her arm.

"I'm … um … yes, the floor seems a little uneven, that's all."

Her eyes were unfocused for a moment, but then she shook her head and bent to the cross.

"The earth trembles, Death defeated groans with the buried one rising," Naomi said quietly. "That's one of the Latin couplets on the shaft." She pointed at the top. "But it's the titulus I came to see especially. Look, where the hand of God is portrayed within a stylized cloud. The Gospels use the phrase, *Jesus of Nazareth, King of the Jews*, but this has *Jesus of Nazareth, King of the Confessors*. It's a very unusual phrase." She bent even closer. "And there, you can just see the line of corrupted Hebrew." She squinted at it. "That's strange, it looks like –"

The curator clapped his hands together, a little gesture of scholarly excitement as he prepared to share more of the story of the artifact.

"It's important to understand the great journey that the

cross has traveled to reach us here. It came to the Met from a Yugoslavian art collector, Ante Topic Mimara, who recovered works of art at the end of the Second World War. He withheld the provenance of the cross, dying with its secrets intact, but there are reports from a Hungarian immigrant that the *crucifixus maledictus* had been seen in the Cistercian monastery of Zirc in the Bakony Mountains in Hungary. It was known as the *crucifixus maledictus* because of one of the carvings, *Maledictus omnis qui pendet in ligno.* Cursed is everyone who hangs on a tree. This refers to the traditional method of crucifixion, and of course Jesus reversed this curse with his sacrifice for us."

Jake bent forward as the curator's voice faded in volume, as if the sound came from beneath a swimming pool. It wasn't unusual to have blocked ears after a flight and he shook his head a little as he tried to catch the words.

"It's thought that the cross was sent to Hungary as part of a ransom for Richard the Lionheart in 1194, when he was captured on his way home from the Crusades. The Abbot of Bury St Edmunds was instrumental in the exchange, with many of the riches of the monastery given in ransom. It's thought that the cross was amongst that treasure."

Light-headed now, Jake swayed slightly. Naomi reached out a hand to steady him, and Jake noticed a few of the academics had moved back to lean against the thick walls.

"The carvings on the cross portray the story of the Passion of Christ," the curator continued, "expressed through the testimony of the evangelists while the Tree of Life winds up the front of the cross. It's stunning even without the missing corpus. The back of the cross … features the individual prophets holding texts from their holy books. They …"

The curator rubbed at his temples as his words trailed off, a confused look crossing his face as he lost track of what he was saying. He clutched the edge of the plinth, turning towards the arched doorway before sinking down to sit on the floor.

Jake felt a lifting sensation, a weightlessness, almost as if he could fly. He wanted to climb up to the top of the Cloisters and jump into the air, sure of his ability to soar like the birds. At the same time, he lost control of his limbs and he sank to his knees, realizing that around him, others were doing the same.

"The tea," Naomi whispered, her voice faint as she dropped to the floor next to him. "They grow *Datura metel* here, downy thorn apple, a powerful hallucinogenic plant used in medieval magic as well as medicine." She looked around at the other academics lying prone on the stone floor, their movements sluggish. "We've been poisoned."

Jake's tongue was thick in his mouth and he couldn't shape a reply as footsteps echoed on the stone floor, two sets deliberately walking towards the room. Jake saw them emerge from the archway in a haze of vision, their features morphing in and out of focus, first lizard like and then shining like angels. He couldn't move his limbs even as his mind seemed to soar above them into the vault of the ceiling. He tried to focus on them, tried to capture aspects of their faces, but he couldn't see properly. They both wore dark cassocks like priests, a uniform that attracted deference and little suspicion in a place like the Cloisters, but they walked like military men.

One of the men carried a suitcase. He laid it on the floor in front of the cross, opening it to reveal a padded interior. He lifted the Cloisters Cross from its stand, reverence in his eyes and in the way he handled it. He pulled it gently, the pieces sliding apart, and he laid each ivory element gently in the case before closing the lid carefully. Ignoring the prone academics on the floor, the pair walked out again, their actions taking only a few minutes. The stone plinth stood empty, the spotlight only serving to emphasize the negative space where one of the great treasures of Christendom had stood so briefly.

CHAPTER 4

THE UPPER BAY SPARKLED and rays of bright sun illuminated the magnificence of the city below. His city. Gilles Noiret never tired of this view, never grew weary of the myriad possibilities that New York could offer those who grabbed for them.

He ran his company from this towering pinnacle, the seventy-second floor of the Chrysler Building. Officially, the escalator finished at the seventy-first floor, but after purchasing the highest levels for his exclusive investment company, Gilles had constructed this sanctuary in the tangle of concrete supports and electrical equipment under the chrome-plated cap of the building. He loved staring out from the Art Deco turret, its silver starburst pattern pointing towards the spire above, with the knowledge that millions of eyes turned towards it every day, orientating themselves by its height and beauty.

Gilles took a tentative breath and felt it catch, sweat prickling as he dreaded the attack to come. He began to cough, a hacking sound that shook his whole body for several minutes.

Clutching his desk, Gilles retched, gasping for air until his lungs released the phlegm that clogged them. He hawked up a glob of bloody mess and spat it carefully into a handkerchief, the warm softness of it in his hand making his stomach clench. It was a piece of him, evidence of his disease. Every time he suffered an attack, he feared it would be his last.

It offended him to be so physically degraded, so broken, and the thought of dying here, choking to death on his own rotting flesh, set his resolve. He had not lived at the pinnacle of wealth to die in the same way as any poor man living rough on the streets. That was not how the American dream was meant to end.

He flipped open his laptop and played the video of the dying nun, her face contorted as she burned. He felt a rising excitement as he watched, the only physical pleasure he could summon as his body rotted from within.

As the video ended, a cloud passed overhead and Gilles caught a reflection of himself in the glass, bent double like an old man. His face was disfigured by the poison he had imbibed just a few years ago at a dinner held by his own brother, meant to kill him so he wouldn't have to share their inheritance. The immigrant sons of Russian and French ancestors, they had taken competition to extremes, both in business and their personal life. But it was Gaspard who had ended that night in the morgue and Gilles had never regretted finishing the brother who had only ever been a rival. There would always be more to compete with in this city of alphas: those with an edge of the blade in their ambition.

Gaspard had left his mark nonetheless, and the dioxin had caused rapid hyperpigmentation. Gilles' once handsome face was marred with patches of darker skin as well as hyperkeratosis, where the skin thickened and became scaly and bumpy. It itched and ached, but the surface ruin was nothing to what the poison had done internally.

In recent months, even the most advanced medicine had failed, so Gilles had sought alternative remedies from the fringes of health and spirituality. He had tried injections made from the tinctures of plants from the deepest Amazon and potions made from endangered animals. He had hired healers of all stripes, from those who chanted and gave him herbs to smoke, to those who told him to look inside and cleanse his soul. He had even paid for *muti*, traditional medicine from South Africa made from body parts. Nothing had worked yet, but he wouldn't give up until his dying breath.

During nights of pain-wracked insomnia, he had ventured into the margins of society, obscure message boards on the dark web – that part of the internet hidden from search engines and accessed via proxy servers. Gilles found things there that turned even his stomach, but he'd also found a glimmer of hope on a religious conspiracy message board that talked of a powerful relic with healing properties.

The group called themselves the Confessors, a word used in the Eastern Orthodox Church to signify a saint who had suffered persecution and torture for their faith, but had not been martyred: someone who suffered in the world but was not yet dead. Gilles understood what those words meant, and that day had begun his quest for the relic. He had pretended piety with the Monseigneur, assuring the Confessors that he only wanted to cleanse his soul and that they would have the relic for their Order. But that blood would be his … and so soon now. It was almost within his grasp. His men had sent word they were on their way from the Cloisters with the cross, and Gilles had not notified the Monseigneur. He would see what they had first.

The intercom buzzed.

Gilles smiled and pressed the button to let the men in, counting the seconds as they ascended in his private elevator.

A knock came on the door and two men dressed in cassocks walked in, their bearing proud in fulfillment of the mission and expectation of reward.

"Any problems?" Gilles said, staying behind his desk to

save his energy even though he was desperate to see inside the case.

"None at all," the man carrying the case said. He set it on Gilles' desk and turned it to face his employer.

Gilles pulled the case towards him. A smile dawned on his face as he beheld the stunning Cloisters Cross, the sunlight making the ivory gleam. He ran a fingertip over the surface, tracing the lines of the Tree of Life, signifying his own resurrection. This time he was close … He had to be.

The Confessors believed that the blood was held within a vial inside the cross. Gilles' heart beat faster as he reached for the shaft with a shaking hand, tipping it over as he lifted it up so he could see within.

The ivory was indeed hollow, but there was nothing inside.

"Where is it?" Gilles whispered. He shook the shaft, coughing with the effort, but nothing fell out. "It's not here!"

His eyes blazed and the two men backed away from his anger, hands raised in supplication.

"Get down to the Sisters of the Guardian Angel," he rasped. "No subtlety this time. I want that vial, whatever it takes."

CHAPTER 5

JAKE ROLLED SIDEWAYS, MUMBLING as he tried to call for help but only succeeding in banging his head on the flagstones. Naomi lay next to him, her dark eyes meeting his, and Jake sensed a calmness in her, a silent message of hope. She had known the name of the herb and if she wasn't concerned, then he was willing to trust her judgement. He breathed more deeply, trying to recall the details of the men who had taken the cross as he waited for the effects to wear off.

It was ten more agonizing minutes before someone came to see why the scholars were so quiet and raised the alarm. The room was soon crowded with medical staff checking the group and the hubbub of gossip. Half an hour later, the victims began to move more freely, the paralysis released as the drug wore off.

Naomi sat up, rubbing her head where she had knocked it against the stone. She turned to look down at Jake and her long dark hair brushed against his hand. The sensation was magnified by his inability to move, and he willed her to lean in closer. Right now, he would be content to lie here all day, and leave the cross for the police. ARKANE didn't deal with theft or even murder, only with the supernatural, and he had seen nothing of that here today, only a very physical crime.

There was concern in Naomi's eyes as she bent over him.

"I guess you drank more tea than I did, but you'll feel alright in a minute." She smiled with encouragement. "Clearly the dosage was meant to render us semi-conscious but not do any permanent damage."

She stood up and walked away to speak with one of the doctors as Jake's strength returned and he pulled himself up to a seated position. A heaviness still pervaded his limbs and his mind was dulled, his hearing still slightly wavering, but the fog was starting to lift now.

"We're cleared to leave," Naomi said, as she returned and crouched next to him. "The museum authorities called the police about the theft and the poisoning. There was a targeted hack on the security cameras just before the cross was taken, so there's no footage of the men."

"Could they be art thieves?" Jake said, rolling his neck until it clicked. With the combination of jet lag and soporific drugs, he seriously needed some more caffeine. "Don't they steal to hire these days?"

"Hmm," Naomi mused as she helped him up, her hand soft on his arm. "I'm not so sure. The chatter we had on the dark web was linked to a group called the Confessors, and given the wording on the cross, it would make sense if they were involved. We should at least look into it a little more back at the office. After all, what else are you doing today?"

She smiled, her eyes flashing with renewed energy, and Jake thought of a few things that might be more fun than tracking down the medieval cross. But he was here for work, and she was a colleague ... as was Morgan, he thought with a trace of guilt. ARKANE didn't make it easy for a relationship to form, that was for sure. Jake followed Naomi back to the car, grabbing another coffee for the ride back downtown.

After negotiating the heavy Manhattan traffic, the car pulled up at the entrance to the United Nations Plaza between First Avenue and the East River, a bastion of international peace and diplomacy in the heart of capitalist individualism. This was a city where such extremes could coexist in a myriad of dimensions. The plot of land was owned by the United Nations, technically extra-territorial although under agreement to follow local, state and federal laws. Jake wondered how many people around here knew of what lay beneath the official buildings, the hidden world of ARKANE.

Security guards verified their IDs at the gate and checked under the car for any devices, pulling open the doors for the sniffer dogs. Like security guards in sensitive places all over the world, these men were professional but unsmiling. Even though they must see Naomi regularly, there was no banter or casual conversation. As they checked the vehicle, Jake looked over at the huge sculpture of a .357 revolver, its barrel knotted in a symbol of non-violence that represented one of the aims of the UN. It was an idealism that Jake appreciated, but he was pretty sure that humanity would never shrug off its destructive side. Nature itself was murderous and every species struggled to survive another day – mankind was just a reflection of that struggle.

He looked further across the plaza to the row of colorful national flags, fluttering in the breeze in front of the main UN building. Jake recognized some of the more obscure countries – Armenia and Belize, Nauru and Uruguay – remembering how his father used to test him years ago. *It's a big world, son*, he would say as they matched countries on a world map to the capital cities and flags of the nations. *You need to know that there's more than this, where the color of someone's skin isn't so important.* As a farmer who had worked the land, his father never ventured out of South Africa, planning to travel on retirement when he expected to hand the farm to his son. A flash of memory and Jake saw the world map on the wall spattered with blood: his father, mother and two sisters butchered by a drug-fueled gang years ago. He took a deep breath, tearing his gaze away from the flags, pushing the grief down as they drove into the underground carpark. He had left those memories behind a long time ago and hadn't expected a resurgence in this distant city.

Naomi drove down several levels, finally pulling into a bay painted with silver lines. At the other end of the floor, the parking bays were marked in blue. Naomi caught Jake's glance at the color coding.

"I know it seems petty," she said, "but a parking space is worth killing over in Manhattan. The UN crowd don't really know what we do on this end, but boy are they precious about their turf. Come on, I'll show you the office."

They entered an elevator, swiped their ID cards and waited for verification of their bio-information before it moved further down. Jake's ears finally cleared in the swift descent. The doors opened a minute later onto the New York office of ARKANE.

It was noisier than the London labs under Trafalgar Square, with the bustle of the city spilling over into the enthusiasm of those who worked here. But the lab areas were set up in a similar way, with glass-walled, temperature-controlled rooms where artifacts were investigated for their supernatural properties.

"I guess you work with objects like this in London?" Naomi paused in front of one of the research bays, where an unusual necklace was strung across a metal stand. A man in a lab coat scraped at it, pushing tiny samples into a test tube.

"I'm usually out in the field, to be honest." Jake squinted at the object. It was made up of animal teeth, beads and shells. "What is this?"

"It's a shaman's necklace originally from Borneo but recovered from a cache in a Queens apartment. What's particularly interesting is the teeth – they don't come from any known species. When boiled they produce the ability to see into other realms. Local legends say the teeth are from dragons in that other universe."

Jake raised an eyebrow, his corkscrew scar twisting.

"Just another day at ARKANE." He grinned. "Gotta love the variety."

"Exactly." Naomi smiled. "Let's get to my office and see what we can find on the cross."

Naomi led Jake past the rows of glass-walled labs and all the way down another corridor, until they reached a little section tucked away from the main area. The word *Linguistics* was displayed on a sign on the door.

"Because I work across so many cases, I get my own room," Naomi said, opening the door to a messy space not much bigger than a cupboard. "Sorry for the chaos – I do know where everything is, honest."

Looking around the room, Jake had a sense that Naomi spent a lot of time here. There was a kettle and toaster on a little fridge and what looked like a rolled-up sleeping bag and travel mat in the corner. Books were stuffed into floor-to-ceiling shelving on one side of the room, their spines showing all kinds of languages, many he didn't even recognize. Did she live for her work, as he did?

Naomi grabbed her laptop and whipped it open. Jake caught a glimpse of her screensaver – an older Native American man's face in profile, looking out over the ocean. Her father perhaps, as she had mentioned Cherokee blood. She opened the ARKANE systems, typing quickly and pulling up some documents for Jake to look at.

"As we were lying there after the cross was taken," she said, "I was thinking about the strange script on the titulus. I think it might be Enochian."

"The language of the angels?"

Naomi nodded. "Supposedly. It was recorded in the occult

journals of John Dee in late sixteenth-century England. It was meant to be the language that Adam spoke with God, and that was used to name all the animals. I guess you could call it a language of creation. Dee was a mathematician and astrologer, advisor to Queen Elizabeth I, with one foot in science and the other in magic."

"But the dates don't match," Jake said. "It's odd that it should be on the cross, considering the age of the carving is way before Dee's time."

Naomi frowned. "I seem to remember something …" She tapped on the laptop, bringing up a copy of the Hermetic work *Monas Hieroglyphica*. "Here, this is one of Dee's great works and he took a copy to Hungary to present to Maximilian, the Holy Roman Emperor. If the cross was in Hungary at the time, it's likely that Dee would have seen such an unusual piece, and that could have been the basis for his own Enochian language."

As she flicked through the virtual book, Jake spotted an image on the edge of one heavily illustrated page. It depicted a glass flask full of ruby liquid.

"Stop there," he said, and Naomi zoomed in, expanding the image. "The chatter that ARKANE picked up mentioned something about the blood of an angel," Jake said. "Can you read the text around it?"

Naomi's lips moved silently as she read the strange text, her dark eyes fixed on the screen. Jake could almost see the workings of her mind as she turned over the words, her body taut as she concentrated.

"It's retelling a legend from the mouth of an angel," she said after a few minutes. "The one who drinks the blood will see into the supernatural realm, and may bargain the drops for whatever they desire. Time and space are nothing for those who stand beyond." She shook her head slowly, a smile dawning on her lips. "That's pretty cool, actually. Do you think that the Cloisters Cross holds this relic?"

"It certainly explains the interest in it," Jake said. "And makes me more concerned about getting it back. What else is significant about the cross?"

"As well as the angelic aspects, the cross is about resurrection, which isn't surprising, but it's done in an unusual way." Naomi retrieved some close-up pictures of the cross. Jake bent closer to the screen, feeling the warmth of her skin near his arm. She smelled of coconut and jasmine, and he couldn't help but lean closer.

"You can see the pruned tree on the shaft," she said. "It's a date palm, the Latin name is *Phoenix dactylifera*. It dies and comes to life again in a similar manner to the phoenix, the bird that rises from the flames."

"So the Tree of Life portrayed as the seat of immortality, like the Fountain of Youth," Jake said.

Naomi nodded, and then pointed at something else on the screen.

"This Tree of Life is mentioned in Genesis, chapter three, *And the Lord God said, 'The man has now become like one of us, knowing good and evil. He must not be allowed to reach out his hand and take also from the tree of life and eat, and live forever.'* But the book of Enoch, which is in the biblical Apocrypha, has a verse which states that in the time of judgement, God will give all those whose names are in the Book of Life fruit to eat from the Tree of Life. The book isn't canonical, so most aren't aware of it, but its only extant copy is in Ge'ez, the language of Ethiopian holy writing, one of the earliest parts of the church."

Jake remembered visiting the Ethiopian Coptic church on the roof of the church of the Holy Sepulchre in Jerusalem in the hunt for the Pentecost stones. Momentarily, he wondered if Morgan was somewhere near there right now, thinking of him on the other side of the world.

A bell chimed, announcing an incoming message. Naomi leaned in to read it.

"There's been a woman reported missing who fits the profile of the crucified victim. A Sister from the Order of the Guardian Angel." Naomi met Jake's eyes.

"Let's head up there," Jake said, grabbing his coat. "And stop by the weapons locker on the way out."

CHAPTER 6

Sɪsᴛᴇʀ Rᴏsᴀʟɪᴇ ʀᴇᴀᴄʜᴇᴅ ᴜᴘ to light the candles at the back of the chapel, her concentration focused on the depth of the flames as they caught. The main door to the street swung open with a creak, the sound echoing through the church. It was a little early for any worshippers to be arriving for the service, but the church was always open as a place of contemplation. In her forty years of service, the city had been a backdrop to her own daily devotions and she welcomed those who worshipped at any time. Sister Rosalie liked to try and guess what people did when they came in, wondering what troubled them and why they sought out the Lord in the middle of their day. She crossed herself and sent up a prayer of thanks that she could serve the community here, then turned and walked to the chapel archway to see who had entered.

Three men strode down the center of the aisle carrying holdall bags, their long dark coats disguising what might be beneath. They walked towards the altar, menace in their echoing footsteps. Sister Rosalie glimpsed one of the men as he passed, his eyes narrowed with a determined expression, his features pinched with a hunger that wasn't of the corporeal kind. She quickly ducked behind a column, hoping she hadn't been seen. Her breath came fast and she stifled it with one hand. These were not penitents seeking the Lord's grace – these were men bent on violence.

After the disappearance of the Reverend Mother, the Sisters of the Order of the Guardian Angel had been reminded of what to do if they were ever under attack. As citizens of New York City, they weren't alone in preparing for invasion, but the nuns were also trained in spiritual warfare. The prayer of the breastplate of Saint Patrick came to Sister Rosalie's lips now. *I armor myself today with the power of the Most Holy Trinity*, she said under her breath.

She peeked out again from behind the column, watching as the men strode towards the doorway that led into the convent area behind the church. The long coat of the man at the back fluttered open and she spotted a handgun in his waistband. As the men stepped through the archway out of sight, Sister Rosalie scurried to the opposite side of the church, where another door led into the convent rooms. Her heart thumped in her chest as she considered how she could help the Sisters within, as well as safeguarding the secret at the heart of the convent. The Reverend Mother had protected it, and now that task fell to her. She pushed open the door carefully and stepped inside, her footsteps almost silent on the marble floors.

A scream came from the rooms beyond, followed by the shouts of the men rounding up the Sisters. A banging noise resounded, as if something had been knocked over. Then, all was quiet. Sister Rosalie pushed away her feelings of guilt as she navigated the hallways towards the inner rooms of the convent. The Sisters would be safe for now. Most of them knew nothing of the relic and the old ones would hold their tongues against the invaders.

The truth behind the name of their order was obscured by over-engineered religious metaphor, but a chosen few were aware of what lay beneath. This great city was protected by the relic of a Guardian Angel, and it was held here in the convent, passed down over the years by women of faith who were able to resist the temptations of what it might offer.

Sister Rosalie reached the tiny chapel on the edge of the private quarters. It was here that the Reverend Mother had visited daily, saying prayers that she reserved for this sacred place. The altar was simple, a rectangular block of stone covered with a white cloth; a carved wooden crucifix on top, the figure of Christ twisted in agony as his eyes beseeched Heaven for release. Two heavy copper candlesticks flanked the figurine.

On the wall behind the crucifix was a wooden cabinet, the real focal point of the room. It was painted with the figures of angels, binding another of their kind in the center. Its face was stricken with guilt and pain, and from its pale flesh, blood flowed onto the earth. Shoots of new life sprang from the dark stain, with tendrils of leaves and buds that bloomed into flowers.

It was faintly blasphemous to think that an angel could supercede the worship of Christ, but legend told of the power of the relic and perhaps that made it more real than the figure of Christ crucified. Sister Rosalie edged around the altar and reached for the cabinet.

"Stop there, Sister." The gruff voice came from behind her, and Sister Rosalie instinctively put her hands in the air, turning around to see who spoke.

It was the first man who had walked into the church, his eyes scanning the chapel around her. Thank the Lord she hadn't yet opened the cabinet. There was still a chance he would move on from this place.

"You're welcome in the Lord's house," she said softly. "But we don't allow laymen in this area. It is reserved for the nuns. Shall we go out into the public area of the main church?"

The man snorted with laughter.

"I don't think so, Sister. It seems you have something here that my boss wants badly. I don't think that would be out in the public area, do you?" He walked towards her, eyes narrowing. "I think it might be in here. If you just stay quiet now, I won't have to hurt you."

Sister Rosalie dropped her head in the very aspect of a devout nun, assuming the mantle of the downtrodden woman of God this man would expect. But her soul burned with the passion of her Lord, her dedication to protecting the heart of the convent, and with the righteous anger of the saints.

The man stepped closer and bent to lift the altarcloth, checking underneath. Sister Rosalie grabbed one of the metal candlesticks and with all her strength, slammed it down on the back of the man's neck. The thud of metal against flesh shocked her but before he could recover from the first blow, Sister Rosalie raised the candlestick again. She couldn't let him up or he would finish her. Grunting with effort, she smashed it down again, her breath mingled with sobs.

The man slumped to the floor, and Sister Rosalie stood over him, her fists tight on the metal raised high above her head. As blood trickled from his unmoving mouth, she dropped the candlestick as if it burned her. It clanged to the floor and rolled to the side of the room. She fell to her knees in front of the altar.

"Oh Lord Jesus, forgive me," she whispered as she crossed herself repeatedly, fearing that she was now tainted with the blood that she had shed.

A scream rang out from the rooms beyond and Sister Rosalie looked up at the sound. It wouldn't be long until the other men came to look for this one. She had to get out of here. Rising again, she went around to the wooden cabinet and opened it, her fingers shaking.

Inside was a glass vial, its clear sides revealing a viscous dark red substance. Was this really the blood of a Guardian Angel, Sister Rosalie wondered, or was it all just a myth?

Another scream and then a moan from the gathered nuns.

"No, please!" The voice was Sister Mary Clare's.

Sister Rosalie froze, the vial in her shaking hands. The young girl was one of the most attractive of the novitiates and her violation would not be difficult for the men. She looked down at the vial. Was this really worth the sanctity of the Sisters? Surely the Lord would desire the protection of his daughters first, the real treasures of the convent?

She glanced down at the prone man. She had already sinned enough today, and her vow to keep the relic safe seemed worthless in the face of real suffering. Her Sisters needed her. She stepped out of the chapel and walked towards the main convent room, the vial clutched in her hand.

She pushed open the door and almost wept at what she saw. Sister Mary Clare was bound, her habit pulled up and one of the men had his hand between her legs, pulling aside her underclothes as he unbuckled his belt. The look of lust on his face was like the fiends of Hell that Brunelleschi had painted on the dome of Florence. The other nuns were herded into a corner, while another man stood with a gun in each hand.

"Tell me where it is," he said, his quiet tone all the more menacing. "Otherwise she'll only be the first to be violated."

"Stop." Sister Rosalie spoke from the doorway, her voice calm with authority. She held the vial up. "This is what you want. Take it and leave us in peace."

The armed man kept his guns trained on the Sisters.

"Check it," he said to the other man, who hesitated a moment, disappointment in his eyes as he left Sister Mary Clare bound on the floor.

Sister Rosalie held the vial out as the man approached.

"This is the blood of the Guardian Angel," she said.

He took it from her hand, holding the vial to the light

and tipping it slightly so the contents swirled inside.

"How do we know it's real?"

Sister Rosalie smiled coldly. "Faith of course, something perhaps your master lacks. This relic has been the heart of the Order for as long as records have been kept." Her eyes flicked to the cowering Sisters, to the weeping Sister Mary Clare on the floor. "But the real heart of the Order is the Sisterhood."

She pushed past the man and knelt next to Sister Mary Clare, pulling the weeping nun into her arms and rocking her back and forth. Sister Rosalie's eyes blazed as she looked up at the invaders. "You have what you came for. Now get out."

The man backed away from the group of nuns, his guns still trained on them.

"If this is some kind of trick, we will be back, Sister."

The other man spoke, his eyes on Sister Mary Clare. "And I'll enjoy finishing what we started."

They turned to leave, but a roar of anger stopped them. Sister Rosalie paled as she realized that she should have carried on beating the man in the chapel. He stumbled along the corridor, his colleagues rushing to help him back into the room.

"You bitch." He pointed the gun at Sister Rosalie with a wavering hand, clicked off the safety and took aim.

CHAPTER 7

"PLEASE." SISTER ROSALIE STOOD, moving away from the rest of the Sisters. "Just take the vial and leave us now."

The man's eyes were manic, pain turning him into a wounded animal, desperate to lash out. For a second, it seemed like he might relent … but then, the sound of a gunshot echoed through the room.

A surprised sigh escaped Sister Rosalie's lips. She saw the panic on the faces of the nuns as they looked at her and a coldness spread through her body. She looked down to see the hole in her habit, the blood on her side. She dropped to her knees, hands clutched at her ribs as the pain blossomed. She gasped, her breath ragged.

The man stepped forward, pressing the muzzle of the gun to her head. Sister Rosalie looked up at him, but she couldn't hate him. The love of the Lord pervaded her now and she whispered a prayer of forgiveness. *They know not what they do, Lord.* The man's eyes flickered, as if he saw beyond her physical form. He hesitated and then turned away.

"She's finished," he growled, looking around at the rest of the nuns. "If the vial is fake, we'll be back for the rest of you."

The men backed out of the room, and then turned to run towards the rear of the building, taking the vial with them.

Some of the nuns crowded round Sister Rosalie, taking her hands and praying as one ran to call an ambulance and others tended to the shocked Sister Mary Clare.

Jake and Naomi stepped into the Church of the Guardian Angel just as a gunshot rang out in the rooms beyond. They both pulled their weapons and ran towards the sound. Jake hesitated at the arched doorway, listening for an indication of what was within. Several pairs of footsteps rushed away from them, and they heard the sound of voices raised in prayer and weeping. Jake pushed open the door and ran down the corridor with Naomi behind him. She pulled her phone from her jacket, calling for backup from the local police.

He glanced into one of the rooms, seeing the group of nuns crowded around one of their own, several on their knees swaying in prayer. They looked up at him in alarm, instinctively bunching together.

"It's okay," he said. "We're friends. Which way did they go?"

Naomi stepped forward into the room, and the nuns relaxed as they saw another woman.

"Out the back," one of the nuns said. "They've taken something. Please – help us."

Jake turned and sprinted towards the back of the convent, his weapon held low in front of him. Ahead, he heard the revving of a vehicle and men's voices. He peered around the corner of the back door as two men pulled a wounded third man into a minivan.

He shot at them, firing twice, hitting one man in the shoulder while the other bullet pierced the side of the vehicle. The men returned fire and Jake ducked back behind the doorway, hearing the chip of bullets into stone. The van accelerated away and Jake ran out after them, firing at the van, hitting it a couple more times before it pulled away, screeching around a corner and out of sight. Police sirens wailed in the distance but it was too late to follow now. There were no plates, but there were enough cameras downtown that they should be able to track it.

Jake turned and headed back into the convent, pausing at the doorway to the room within. Naomi knelt with the nuns in the center of the room, where one woman lay in a pool of blood. Naomi looked up, her eyes filled with tears.

"This is Sister Rosalie," she said. "They shot her and took the relic of the Guardian Angel."

Jake knelt next to the woman as the prayers of the gathered nuns rang loud around them. The wound in Sister Rosalie's side pulsed blood onto the marble floor of the chapel, despite the wad of bandaging that one of the other nuns held against it. She gasped for breath, her eyes unfocused.

"It's OK," Jake whispered, tears pricking his eyes at her suffering. So often he survived the aftermath of violence, arriving too late to stop it. "We've got you now. You're going to be alright. The ambulance is almost here."

Naomi reached forward and stroked the hair from the nun's forehead.

"God is with you," she whispered softly to the nun, with a faith in her voice that Jake didn't have. He felt a pang of something like envy that Naomi could believe and find comfort in something beyond this earthly life.

The nun lifted her hand towards the light above her, reaching for the coffered ceiling. Her eyes were fixed on a point beyond the physical realm and Jake hoped she could see a better life ahead. Then she turned her head, her eyes clear as a summer sky after rain, a realization dawning in her eyes.

"Follow the angel," she whispered.

Her eyes closed and Jake felt her body sag, the life leaving it even as her physical remains lay still in his arms. He laid the nun gently on the ground, putting a prayer cushion under her head as the other Sisters gathered around to mourn.

Jake and Naomi rose to let them tend to her body, walking to the doorway.

"At least she wasn't afraid of death," Naomi said. "Her faith gave her strength and a hope for the afterlife."

Jake wanted to voice his lack of belief, his surety that there was only the void after this. This minute was all they had, this day the only one they could live and there was nothing beyond. But he just nodded, feeling a sense of isolation at his unbelief in this house of God.

"They took the relic," Naomi said, turning to look back at the nuns. "And the people who did this must also have the Cloisters Cross."

Jake nodded. "I'm going after them ..." He left the opening for her, unsure as to whether a deskbound agent with little field experience would want to dive further into this mission. Morgan would have jumped at the chance, but she was halfway across the world.

Naomi crossed herself, ducking her head towards the altar and then turned. There was fire in her eyes and Jake saw echoes of an ancestry riven with conflict. This woman wouldn't run from a fight.

"This is my patch, Jake, but you're welcome to join me on the hunt." She walked towards the convent door, Jake following as their footsteps echoed in the nave. "I know where to start. Here in New York, there's only one famous angel that springs to mind."

***

Across the city, in a lab buried deep under the Chrysler Building, Gilles Noiret paced back and forth. The men had brought the vial straight to the underground carpark, and he had rushed it to his private lab. They had been trying to find a cure for his illness for years, and now the equipment would be used to test what was in the vial.

The Monseigneur would hear of the theft all too soon and would demand access. Gilles had to be quick. He had wanted to drink the liquid then and there, take the risk on what it might do. But his fear of poison was so great that everything had to be tested before it reached his lips. This vial was no different.

A scientist in a lab coat used a pipette to extract several samples of the dark red liquid, putting it into test tubes and one on a slide to examine under the microscope.

"How long will this take?" Gilles barked at the scientist. "I must know what it is."

"Of course," the scientist whispered, his concentration fixed on the liquid. "The preliminary tests won't take long."

He loaded the test tubes into various machines, starting the processes to test the blood. Then he bent to the microscope, putting the slide under the lens.

"Hmm," the scientist said, standing up straight again.

"What? What is it?" Gilles demanded.

"It's definitely blood. It looks to be from some type of animal though. I don't see any obvious anomalies that would make it anything special."

One of the machines beeped and the scientist went to check the computer screen next to it for the results.

"As I thought. The DNA shows that the blood is from a type of goat that is only found natively in France. It's certainly old, several centuries in fact. But I'm sorry sir, I can't see what efficacy this would have if drunk."

Gilles spun around, fists clenched. He felt the tightness in his chest begin to spasm at the onset of a coughing fit. Desperation rose within him, a faith born of a belief that he could cheat death – that he would not be subject to the laws of humanity. His wealth ruled this city and he would not go out with a last rotting breath.

He snatched up the vial on the bench, ripping the glass top from it. He lifted it to his lips and drank the contents, gulping the coppery taste down, forcing himself to swallow the thick liquid.

The scientist gasped, his eyes crinkling with disgust.

Gilles turned to grab a tissue and caught sight of his own face in a mirrored flask on the bench, a hideously scarred and puckered visage with a mouth painted in the blood of a long-dead animal. He pulled a tissue from a pack and wiped his mouth, the crimson stain all that was left of the so-called relic.

There was still hope that the blood had some power. He would not let this be the end. Gilles sat down heavily, waiting for some kind of reaction, hoping for some kind of miracle. The threatening cough subsided but the blood sat heavy in his stomach. Nausea made him want to retch it up, but he kept swallowing to keep it down, breathing deeply to calm himself.

"Water," he barked. The scientist grabbed a bottle from the fridge and handed it over wordlessly. Gilles chugged the liquid down, washing the metallic taste from his throat. There was no feeling other than his own revulsion at drinking the blood. After several minutes passed with nothing, not even light-headedness, Gilles put his head in his hands. He massaged his temples, willing his rising rage to subside.

"What else are you working on?" he asked the scientist, his voice tightly controlled. "Do we have any other options?"

The scientist walked briskly to his desk and pulled out a few printed pages.

"There's an experimental therapy that we can look at. It shows a muted but still positive response in some subjects."

Gilles stood. "Get it, whatever it costs."

He went to his private lift and headed back up to the

penthouse, disappointment flooding him, anger at his own stupid hopes of a miraculous cure. He would send the Monseigneur and his pathetic Confessors packing, their myth turned to ashes in his mouth.

But as he walked into the apartment, a ray of sun peeked through the clouds, illuminating the Cloisters Cross. The sunlight hit the empty shaft, where the corpus of Christ should hang. The legends told that the corpus was the true home of the relic, and the vial had been found alone, with no ivory body of Christ as its resting place. Perhaps the nuns had lied or perhaps they didn't even know that what they'd had was the blood of an old goat. But the corpus was still out there – as long as that was true, there was still hope.

Gilles took his phone out of his pocket, dialing quickly.

"Follow whoever leaves the convent. This isn't over yet."

CHAPTER 8

THE SOUND OF GOSPEL music came from the passage that led under Bethesda Terrace. The voices of a young black choir soared in glory and the acoustics of the space resonated with harmonies. Jake noticed one young woman, her dreadlocks tied back with a red scarf and her arms lifted to the ornate ceiling above. As she sang, she stepped in time with the choir, their simple choreography a way to bring the body into worship. For a moment, Jake was taken back to the townships in South Africa, when as a child he had always been jealous of the way the black community sang with such abandon, such joy. His own white church had been a place of dull song with no passion, a controlled droning that seemed intent on crushing the lively spirit.

Naomi sang a few lines of the tune as they walked past and danced a little, joining the choir in a moment that transcended the pain they had just witnessed at the convent.

"You have a lovely voice," Jake said, noting how her face lit up and her body relaxed as she moved, a glimpse of the woman behind the agent's facade.

"Years of Pentecostal worship," Naomi said, with a smile that spoke of deep contentment. "I'm not exactly a committed believer these days, but boy, do I love the music. I think that many people just go to church to sing and experience the bliss of communal voice. Whether the Lord gave us music, or whether we found it ourselves, it surely is one of the best ways to open the mind to something more than the mundane."

They walked out onto the stone terrace in front of the most famous angel in New York, the Angel of the Waters, standing tall over the large fountain. The bronze figure looked as if she had just touched down from a heavenly descent, one arm out to bless those who came here seeking help. Her wings were outstretched and currently a roost for a number of pigeons that sat atop the sculpture, preening their feathers in the sun. Groups of tourists snapped pictures of the scene as a clamor of bike bells filled the air. A group of tour riders arrived, their guide gesticulating as he explained the fountain's origin within Central Park.

"She's meant to be the angel from the gospel of John, chapter five," Naomi said. "An angel would come down and stir the waters of the pool of Bethesda. Any who entered after the blessing would emerge healed. I think that many come to New York wanting the same miracle in their lives – a resurrection of sorts, or a rebirth."

"What do you expect to find here?" Jake asked, looking around.

Naomi shrugged. "I'm not so sure, to be honest, but this is the most well-known angel in the city. With the Enochian language on the cross and so many angelic references, I have to think that this is connected somehow. Let's at least check it out."

They walked around the perimeter of the fountain, navigating the throngs of tourists taking photos and lovers kissing on the edge, fingers entwined in the water. There were coins in the fountain, thrown in for wishes perhaps. Jake fumbled in his pocket for a quarter and leaned over the water. He let it slip under, sending out a thought for Morgan, hoping that she was safe. Perhaps she was even thinking of him too.

Applause rippled out from the passage and the choir emerged for a break between sets. A couple of members from the group lit cigarettes and turned their faces to the beaming sun as they reveled in the beautiful day. Another sold CDs to the appreciative tourists who had gathered to listen. Jake noticed the young woman with dreadlocks and the red scarf emerge with a backpack. She looked around at the fountain and scanned the crowd. She caught Jake's eye and walked towards them, waving a little.

"Hi," she said. "Don't worry, I'm not asking for anything."

Jake laughed. "I thought your performance was excellent. I'd be happy to put some money in the hat."

"Can we help you with anything?" Naomi said, stepping closer.

The young woman smiled and pulled out her cell phone.

"Actually, I think I'm here to help you. I'm Regina – I just got a text message. I can't say from who, but she says you did something to help the Order of the Guardian Angel this morning."

Naomi's face was serious. "We've just come from the convent. How do you know about them?"

"The Order has lay sisters like me all over the city who serve the community any way we can. I mostly work on the streets – I was a homeless junkie when one of the Sisters found me five years ago. I thought she was an angel, actually." Regina pointed up at the fountain statue. "Just like our angel here, the Sister held out a hand and saved me. Now, I try and help others."

"That sounds fantastic," Jake said. "But we're not looking for salvation."

Regina nodded. "The relic – I know about it. We all do. It's one of those 'matter-of-faith' things to most associated with the Order, but maybe it's based on historical truth way back. Anyhow, my contact has asked me to take you to a place that might help you figure out where the relic is."

"Sounds like a plan," said Jake. "Let's grab a cab."

Regina shook her head. "Actually, it's a little more complicated than that. Where we're going isn't exactly open to the public – and you won't find this route on any GPS."

Naomi raised an eyebrow. "That sounds intriguing."

Regina looked her up and down, eyeing the tailored trousers and jacket. "It is. But girl, how much do you love that suit?"

***

After winding through Central Park, Regina led Jake and Naomi down a zigzag of side streets until they reached an area that even Jake wouldn't want to visit at night.

"Where are we going?" Naomi asked as they walked.

"It's more about how we're getting there," Regina replied with a smile. "I dated a sandhog once. He showed me a lot of the tunnels under the city."

"Sandhog?" Jake asked.

"I guess you could call them urban miners, construction workers who spend their lives underground – boring tunnels, building ducts for new projects, excavation, making sure the water pipes are OK. There's a lot that goes on under this city." She paused by a grate on the sidewalk, pulling a tire iron from her backpack. "Of course, if we're found, we'll get arrested. But just act like this is normal and no one will even notice." She grinned, a feral look coming into her eyes, and Jake caught a glimpse of the girl who had once survived on these streets.

Regina glanced around quickly. There were no cop cars in sight. With one smooth movement, she wedged the end of the tire iron into the grating and heaved it up. She pulled it sideways to reveal a metal ladder leading down into darkness.

"Quickly now," she said. "Wait for me at the bottom."

Jake looked at Naomi and shrugged, then stepped on the ladder and descended. The light dimmed as he went down, his footsteps echoing on the rungs. The sound of dripping water intensified as he reached the bottom. He pulled out his phone and used the torch function to look around. The tunnel was six feet at the tallest point so he would have to crouch to walk through it, and there was shallow water running along the concrete bottom. It smelled earthy with a metallic tang, but underneath there was a hint of the rotting decay and sewage that flowed through these tunnels somewhere.

Naomi stepped down from above and Jake resisted an urge to help her descend the last few rungs. His South African upbringing could sometimes be misconstrued as sexism and he had a suspicion that both these women were more than capable of looking after themselves.

"This is so cool," Naomi said as she looked around, wiping her hands on her tailored suit, oblivious to the dirt. Her eyes were bright in the torchlight. "I've always wanted to come down here, but all the official tours are waaaay too boring."

A clang came from above as Regina pulled the grating back over the hole and then came down to join them. She pulled a pair of gloves and a powerful headtorch from her backpack and put them both on.

"Sorry I don't have more gear for you, but this was a short-notice thing. We don't have too far to go anyway, so your phone batteries should last as torchlight. This way."

Regina stepped into the side tunnel, staying on one side to avoid the water channel. Her left hand touched the wall lightly with sure fingertips, as if the brickwork were braille and its message only for those of the underground world. The walls were brick blocks, like a prison or an institution, but Regina's body became more relaxed down here, and she exuded a sense of freedom. *Perhaps she was more free down here*, Jake thought as he walked hunched over. It was simple to follow the law when you had money and security, but when life was more extreme, when survival was on a toppling edge, it was sometimes easier to live away from prying eyes.

They walked in silence for a few minutes, the sounds of the tunnel becoming more intense: dripping water from the roof above, the burble of the water channel at their feet, the scurrying and scratching of the rats that made their home down here. Then, suddenly a clang from behind them.

Regina stopped, her head whipping round to look back behind Jake. He saw terror in her eyes, residual fear from her previous life.

"That's strange," she whispered after a moment. "I've never known anyone else use that entrance and there's no scheduled maintenance in this part of the tunnels this month. I know the rotation." She frowned. "I'm sure it's nothing. Let's keep moving."

Jake felt the familiar prickle of hair rising on the back of his neck as his senses heightened. Naomi had a hand on her gun and he pulled his own weapon silently, holding it next to his phone. Had they been followed from the convent down here?

They continued down the tunnel, emerging into a wider shaft with ledges that were high enough above water to remain dry most of the year. On one of the ledges, a lounge chair with an ashtray on the arm sat next to a few boxes – a makeshift living room in this strange oasis of dark calm. Above the chair, unreadable bulbous letters in faded paint proclaimed existence below the skin of the street. Mankind has always marked its place upon the earth, from the earliest cave dwellers to these more modern troglodytes.

"I knew the man who based himself here," Regina said. "He was already old when I met him, and older still when someone turned him in to the authorities because he was sick. He cried when they took him away to hospital. I think he wanted to die down here, where he felt free. Up above, people tell you what to do, how to behave. I know it's hard to believe, but some people prefer this to the shelters." She paused, looking around. "Down here used to be my home. I knew all the ways to escape in the dark, but most of the predators are up top anyway."

Regina took another small tunnel that led off from the large one, twisting and turning until Jake was sure he would never be able to find his way back. In his younger days, he could track through dense bush where all the trees looked the same and still navigate to a water hole. But here … he shivered. How many skeletons lay forgotten in this warren of tunnels under the city? How many had become lost and died alone, clawing at the walls?

They stopped by a manhole with a small square grating on the top.

"We've got to go down quite a long way now," Regina said, shining her torch down into the hole below. "The entrance is off this access shaft, which as far as I can tell hasn't been used since they built the lower tiers of the place."

She pulled the tire iron out again and hooked the cover to pull it away. Naomi bent to help.

"You still haven't told us where we're going," she said.

Regina grinned. "I think you're gonna like it when we get there."

CHAPTER 9

JAKE FOUND THE ACCESS shaft a little too tight for comfort. It was a square chimney just wider than a man's shoulders – a small man's shoulders – and he was over six feet and broad with it. He concentrated on breathing deeply, focusing on the brickwork in front of him as he mechanically stepped down the ladder after the two women.

He could hear Naomi and Regina chatting below, the echoes of their laughter filtering up to him. Naomi seemed to find these dark places a natural habitat, her smart suit forgotten as she had enthusiastically followed Regina down the shaft. If they were being followed, it would be easy to find them with this level of noise. He paused for a moment to reach around his back and check the gun was still safely tucked there before he continued down. After a few more minutes, he found Naomi and Regina standing in an alcove off the main shaft in front of a metal access hatch.

"Welcome to the New York Public Library," Regina said with a broad grin. "It has seven floors of stacks but the official plans don't show the sub-basement where some of the city's most politically sensitive documents are kept. The treasures and rare manuscripts are above, but down here are the secrets. We'll be entering directly into that area."

Jake's mind flashed to the ARKANE vaults, buried deep

under Trafalgar Square in central London, way below the transport level and the pipework necessary to run the city. Could those levels be accessed in the same way? It was something to talk to Director Marietti about when he got back to London.

"Oh, wow!" Naomi said, her eyes shining with excitement. "I've heard rumors of this level but I've never been able to get in, even with ARKANE access."

"What are we looking for here?" Jake asked. "And how does it relate to the relic?"

Regina began to turn the wheel on the hatch, opening the lock that held it shut.

"The Mother Superior of the Order of the Guardian Angel has always been a prominent figure in the city," she said. "In the background, for sure, but influential in her own way. Those who held the position have always written diaries and those records are locked here in the vault because of the secrets that the Mother Superiors have always kept. My source at the convent said that the last recorded sighting of the original relic was around 1890, so we'll be trying to find the diary from that time."

Regina pulled the door and it swung silently open on oiled hinges. She put her finger on her lips as they stepped inside, motioning them into silence. Directly in front of the door was a huge wooden slab, the back of a giant bookcase or storage unit. Regina inched into the space behind it while Naomi easily followed and Jake squeezed along after them. Regina peeked her head around the end. After a moment, she stepped into the room, beckoning for them to emerge.

"It's OK," she said. "There's no one here. There never is, actually, and I've been coming here for years. It's always this awesome temperature, keeps you warm in the winter and there doesn't seem to be any security to worry about. I think they've forgotten about this place. The last documents deposited down here are dated 1972."

The vault had a low ceiling and rolling shelves that stretched into darkness ahead of them, creating a sense of intimacy. The sound of their voices was muted by the stacks of paper, books and documents that lay filed on the shelving. The place smelled of age and knowledge, crumbling into dust, for life was a constant fight against entropy, the degeneration of all things. It looked like some of the archives here had already succumbed. Jake thought of Martin Klein's database back in London, and how much his friend would love to get hold of what was in this vault. It could be a possibility later, but for now Jake walked to the first shelf and scanned the contents, written in spidery handwriting on an index card taped to the end.

"Do you have any sense where the diaries might be?" Jake asked. "We don't have time to go through the whole vault."

"Of course," Regina said. "I searched for them after I became part of the Sisterhood." She walked down the narrow aisle, Naomi and Jake following behind until they reached a particular aisle. Regina pulled a cord to turn on the light in the stack. The illumination was dim but it was better than their torches. She turned the handle to open up the rolling stack, revealing a row of identical black books standing upon the shelves, each one with a date etched in gold on the spine. Year upon year of diaries, each one an inch thick.

Jake raised an eyebrow. "This could be a problem."

"We just need to narrow down the date range," Naomi said, trailing her fingers along the spines as she scanned the dates. "As much as I'd love to sit and read these earlier tomes, we should start with the year the relic was seen and go from there. We'll scan for mentions of it and hope the Mother Superior wrote about it." She pulled the book from 1890 off the shelf and a cloud of dust lifted into the air. "You take this one, Jake." She handed it to him, coughing as the dust settled on her skin and clothes.

Regina pulled down the next one in the series. "I'll look at this one."

Naomi took the following year and they all sat on the floor, books on their laps. The sound of pages turning was soon the only thing that could be heard, their breathing more rhythmic as they settled into the search.

Jake's diary was a monotonous account of life in the convent, with lists of ailments amongst the nuns, accounting notes and snippets of information on visitors. Page after page of this made his attention wander as the minutes ticked by. He glanced up at Naomi, who leaned against the stack behind her, dark eyes fixed on the page, her slim fingers gently laid on the ivory paper. She was attractive above ground in her bureaucrat's suit and perfect hair, but she was stunning down here covered in the dust and dirt of adventure. She looked up and caught his gaze, a smile playing around her full lips.

"Found anything?" she said, her voice soft.

"Convent admin mainly," Jake replied. "You?"

"This could be interesting. The Mother Superior has started to visit an asylum and she speaks of women there needing divine protection. It's located –"

Her words were cut off as a dull clang came from the end of the vault, back where the access hatch led to the shaft.

"Get back," Jake whispered, rising quickly and pulling his weapon. Pushing Regina to the back of the rolling stack, he peered around the end of the row, Naomi right next to him, her weapon drawn. Jake's pulse raced as he considered their options. This was the worst environment for a gun fight. There was no other exit they could use and from what Regina had said, they would not be heard even if the place was burning down. He glanced around at the paper surrounding them. And this place would burn indeed.

For a moment, there was silence.

Then, the unmistakeable noise of a heavy object landing

in the aisle near them, and a grenade rolled into view. There was no smell and no visible smoke, but a hissing noise betrayed the leaking gas.

Jake didn't hesitate. He yanked off his jacket and threw it over the grenade, dampening the gas down, but he knew it wouldn't hold the chemical for long. "Get to the end, as far away as you can," he said. "Run, now."

He sprinted in the opposite direction, back towards the hatch they had come through, where whoever had thrown the grenade must surely be. As he reached the back of the bookcase, he looked round the corner quickly. He saw the back of a man's blue jacket and one leg as he stepped into the hatch.

Jake drew his gun and took a shot, knowing he wouldn't be able to get through fast enough. The man grunted but pulled through, the shot catching only his jacket. Jake squeezed into the space, fighting to get to the door, but as he reached it, he heard the unmistakeable sound of the wheel lock being spun into place.

He pounded on the metal.

"You coward," he shouted. "Come in here and face me in person."

He banged the door one last time and then swore, a torrent of Afrikaans that wasn't fit for translation. He squeezed back through the gap and into the vault again. Covering his mouth with his shirt sleeve, he crouched low to the floor and crawled back towards the stacks, beginning to feel the edges of his vision go dim. It made Jake angry to think he might die like a librarian instead of a warrior – not the way he had planned to go at all.

"Back here, Jake," Naomi called. The two women had crawled right to the back of the corridor, as far as they could get from the source of the smoke. Regina lay with her head in Naomi's lap, her eyes closed, her breathing shallow. The Mother Superior's diary was next to them.

"She succumbed quickly," Naomi said, coughing as she spoke. "We should never have brought her into this. There's been too much death already today."

Jake sat down next to her and she leaned her head on his shoulder. He reached one hand up to stroke her hair.

"Well, passing out twice in one day next to you isn't so bad," he said.

Her laugh was soft and she lifted her head. He turned to look into her dark eyes.

"I hope we can manage it again sometime."

Moments later, the world shifted and Jake slipped away into darkness.

CHAPTER 10

JAKE OPENED HIS EYES to a hazy view of the stacks, illuminated by a nimbus around the light next to them. His head pounded and nausea rose within him, but as he came fully alert, he realized that the gas had been merely to knock them out. The Mother Superior's diary was gone, as were both his and Naomi's guns, but it looked like nothing else had been touched. Maybe whoever did this didn't want to leave bodies as evidence that would point to the stolen diary. This way, no one would be any the wiser about the incursion.

Naomi's head rested on Jake's shoulder and he was acutely aware of her soft body against his. Her breathing was natural and she stirred a little. Her dark hair smelled of coconut shampoo and he closed his eyes for a moment, inhaling her scent. Regina's head still lay in Naomi's lap and she looked like she was breathing more easily, her skin a normal color. Jake reached down to check her pulse, relieved to find it steady and strong. He shook Naomi's shoulder gently.

"Hey … wake up," he said, softly. "You OK?"

She sighed and lifted her head, taking a deep breath as she focused on the vault and rubbed her eyes.

"Regina," she said, bending to the young woman in concern.

"She'll be alright in a minute," Jake said. "It looks like we were only drugged for the short term while they took the diary. We'll make sure she gets some help when we get out of here."

Naomi looked up at him with a dawning smile.

"That must mean that the book really does hold the location of the relic, and I think I read about it before the gas attack. I know where we need to go next."

***

"You can take the boat out into the Sound but just don't land on any of the islands," the skipper said as Jake signed the paperwork. "It's illegal and they're really strict about it. You do not want to cross the Corrections Department, believe me."

"We just want to do a little sightseeing," Jake said. "Maybe some night fishing later on."

The skipper frowned.

"Not really the weather for it but hey, it's your call. The insurance is all in order." He stamped the documents and filed them quickly, locking away the cash Jake had provided. There were a couple of extra hundred-dollar notes in the pile after his questioning glances at their dusty and dirty clothes, evidence of the underground excursion.

After Regina had roused from the drugged sleep, they'd traced their way back through the tunnels and left her at the ER, where she assured them she would be fine. Then, Jake and Naomi continued the hunt alone. They had two backpacks now, delivered at short notice by an ARKANE agent from the central office. Their weapons and torches had been replaced, just in case, but they still wore the clothes from the day's adventure.

Together, they headed out for the dock, the skipper

leading the way. He showed Jake the controls of the boat, explained the safety features and wished them a good evening. Naomi helped cast off and they set out north from City Island towards Chimney Sweeps and the Blauzes, where there was apparently some good fishing.

As soon as they were far enough away, Jake turned the boat east towards Hart Island. The throb of the engine through his feet and the movement of the ocean made him smile. Being out here in the wind was far preferable to the dark tunnels beneath the city. He took a deep breath of the salty air. Naomi sat at the bow, her dark hair tied back with a few strands caught by the breeze.

"Some call it the island of the outcasts," she said, her voice wistful as they caught sight of the shoreline ahead. "It was originally a prisoner of war camp for Confederate soldiers – it's functioned as a juvenile prison workhouse, a quarantine camp for yellow fever, a missile base, a hospital for tuberculosis patients, and of course, a lunatic asylum."

"And now?" Jake asked, steering the boat across the bay, his hand steady on the wheel.

"It's a mass burial ground for those unclaimed and unknown. Those without a name, or those with a name but no one to bury them. Those too poor to afford a proper grave. Babies who died in hospital or were abandoned. There are over 800,000 people buried here. The graves are dug by the inmates of Rikers Island who come by ferry every day."

Jake thought of Morgan and their visit to the mummy crypt of Palermo, where the baby room had been the most disturbing place. He shook his head with a sigh.

"Mass graves aren't exactly my idea of a fun tourist day out, you know."

"Sorry." Naomi smiled. "But the Mother Superior's diary specifically mentioned this place. She used to minister to the women here at the asylum. Her words were something like, *the relic will protect those who suffer here. They deserve it more than the rich languishing in the towers built from the bodies of those they exploit."*

"Ouch," Jake said. "She sounds like a firebrand."

"Just the type to buck tradition and bring the relic here perhaps. The diary must be important or it wouldn't have been taken."

Jake scanned the waters around them.

"Indeed, but it does mean that we might have some company soon."

"It's near impossible to get permission to come onto the island," Naomi said. "Even those who find relatives buried here have to go through the prison administration system. Then if you get permission, you're restricted to the ferry dock gazebo where the burial records are held."

"So we have no choice but to trespass, right?"

"Absolutely none." Naomi turned and her eyes were bright, her smile alive with enthusiasm. "Besides, where would the fun be in going through the usual channels? I'm having a pretty exciting time with you, Jake Timber. Trespassing twice in one day. I really have to get out of the office more often."

As they neared the shore, they looked for a place to land the boat, avoiding the official pier where there would likely be cameras. The island was low with sparse cover. Just a few trees, scrub and patches of dust. It was unkempt, as if those who came here couldn't leave fast enough. Buildings dotted the landscape but all were rundown, used as storehouses while they still stood, but they looked as if they would be left to crumble or soon be leveled to make room for new graves. There was a sense of abandonment, a place only inhabited by ghosts and the dead.

Jake slowed the engine as they scanned the shoreline, avoiding the treacherous reefs. Signs dotted the perimeter on the rocks above the shallow beaches. *New York City Corrections Department. Restricted area. No trespassing. No docking. No anchoring. Violators will be prosecuted.*

"I'm not intending to violate anything," Jake said. "How 'bout you?"

"Certainly not," Naomi said. "How about landing over there?"

She pointed out a cobbled beach under the shadow of an imposing building with a tall chimney, the ruins of the island's power plant. Jake steered the boat in, revving slightly before pulling up the motor so they could coast up the stones a little. Naomi jumped gracefully out onto the shore, holding the boat steady so Jake could disembark. They dragged the boat further away from the water line, the sound of metal on stone loud in the still air.

"No point in trying to hide the boat," Jake said. "If we get caught, it's better to be clueless tourists than clandestine operatives."

Naomi pulled a map from her backpack and peered closely at it, turning it around until she got her bearings.

"OK, the asylum isn't too far. This way."

They walked up from the beach through the trees, stepping quietly with an instinctive respect. It was a place that demanded silence, as if to wake what slumbered here would be abomination. The ground was covered in patchy mist and Jake fancied that the souls of the unloved clung to the earth, seeking solace. What is heaven if you have no hope of seeing those who made life on earth so happy? He thought of his parents, his sisters, murdered too young. He didn't really believe in an afterlife, but in quiet moments, he could sense their presence and there was still hope that he might be together with them in the end.

A red brick building loomed from the trees, with tall window spaces that gaped black inside. The map named it as the Pavilion Building, which had once housed the Hart Island Lunatic Asylum, a women-only residence that held the overflow from Blackwell Island Insane Asylum.

"They only brought chronic cases here," Naomi said. "Perhaps the ones who couldn't be treated, so they kept them somewhere their screams wouldn't disturb the public."

"And where the so-called civilized didn't have to deal with them," Jake said.

The forest floor grew right to the doorstep of the building, green shoots withering as they touched the brick as if afraid to cross the threshold. It was quiet and still, with no sound of birdsong or rustle of animals in the overgrown foliage. The ambient noise was only the far-off city and the ocean waves that washed all the way to the Atlantic. The air was damp, clinging to their skin, and the smell of the forest had crept in here, nature slowly reclaiming that which man had left behind. Jake willed the encroachment on faster, for perhaps only when this place was a crumble of ruins would the shades of these women be at peace.

He stepped inside with Naomi following close behind. The structure was falling apart, the inner layers of the original building showing through. The years of weathering had stripped the paint and paper from the walls, revealing the struts and planks. The floor was cracked through repeated floods and winter cold. Piles of dead leaves had blown in through glassless windows. The place was clad in decaying shades of brown and green, natural colors that dominated as the traces of human touch were slowly, but inevitably, erased.

They walked onwards. In one room, four metal beds stood against a wall regulation-distance apart, rusted and surrounded by fallen masonry. In another, three plain wooden caskets sat next to planks and plastic gloves, waiting for the bodies that would be laid inside. What kind of a life would it have been, incarcerated here and then buried in these crowded graves? Jake shivered and turned away.

"Maybe there are some records upstairs?" he said.

They walked up to the second floor, their footsteps eerie

in the quiet place, and turned into the first room on the left.

"Oh." Naomi let out a soft gasp at what she saw.

CHAPTER 11

Jake put out a hand to grip the doorframe as a distinct memory came to him. In his younger days in the military, he had been part of a peacekeeping force sent to Rwanda in the aftermath of the genocide. The piles of clothing and shoes on the edge of mass graves were all that was left of the Tutsi people, butchered with machetes and farm tools. Those piles in turn had echoes of Auschwitz and the Nazi death camps … and this room, the floor deep with shoes that seemed to have no owner. Whatever the color of a person's skin, it seemed that humanity would always seek to destroy those viewed as Other.

"Are you OK?" Naomi's voice broke through Jake's reverie.

He let out a deep breath. "Yes … sorry. I was just remembering something that happened a long time ago."

"I know this looks like the aftermath of atrocity," she said. "But actually the inmates used to make shoes as some kind of occupational therapy. They left all this here when they closed the asylum."

Jake shook his head, his smile hiding the turmoil inside. "I can't help but jump to the wrong conclusion. You've got to admit – it's a pretty awful sight. Somehow more disturbing than a load of bodies. But it looks like there's nothing up here. Let's check outside before it gets too dark."

They walked around the perimeter between the wards to the west and came upon a burial pit lying open like a dark maw in the earth.

"Some bodies have apparently been disinterred," Naomi said. "If they can be identified by relatives, they can be reburied somewhere easier to visit."

Jake peered down into the hole, the edges of plain wooden coffins visible under a thin layer of earth, each marked with a scrawled number in black ink.

"Burn me," he said. "I want none of this lying beneath the earth business. The idea of bodily resurrection has always freaked me out."

Naomi giggled. "A little too much like the *Living Dead* for my liking, too. I wouldn't want to be over here for the zombie apocalypse, that's for sure."

There was a sound in the distance and Jake put his hand out, motioning for Naomi to be silent. It was a car engine coming their way.

The pair ran swiftly to cover at the side of the building, ducking behind a ruined wall so they still had a view of the overgrown road. A battered truck pulled up and two men got out. One was younger, good looking. The other was a grim-faced boxer type in a blue jacket, who slung a shovel over his shoulder as they emerged from the vehicle. They spoke in fast French and Jake was only able to make out one word: *tombe* – the French for grave.

Jake pulled Naomi down behind the wall.

"The guy on the right," he whispered. "I think he was in the vault. I didn't see his face, but that jacket looks familiar."

"We should follow them," Naomi said quietly. "They look like they know more than we do at this point."

Jake nodded. They checked their weapons and left the bulky packs by the wall. With Naomi following close behind, Jake slipped around the side of the building, staying far enough back not to be seen as he peeked through cracks in the structure to keep the men in sight. Soon the men stopped and put their tools down, with the young man checking a GPS location on his phone.

Near where the men stood was a verdant patch of green distinct from the brown surrounds, evidence of life blooming from those buried beneath. The man in the blue jacket tugged a map from his pocket and then bent to examine some small white markers. He grunted with a nod and the pair began to dig.

"We need to get into those trees," Jake whispered, nodding at the copse near the men. "We can't stay here or we won't see what they find."

Naomi turned and stepped quietly away, careful as she walked around the masonry and debris on the ground near the buildings. There was no hesitation in her gait and Jake noticed that she was more confident now, as if she had grown into her agent self during their day together. Still, Jake missed having a partner he could read like a book, whose every action he could anticipate because it would be his own. He missed Morgan, but he still had doubts that she would want him back as a partner, damaged as he was in body and mind. He followed Naomi quietly, resolve rising within him. He wouldn't let her down today – he was still a soldier, an ARKANE agent, a man she could rely on. He straightened his back and inhaled slowly, filling his lungs with the air of the forest and easing the tension from his limbs. He was ready, whatever might come.

The pair slipped through the trees, navigating a wide circle within hearing distance of the men, who spoke softly as they dug. It seemed like the older man was complaining, even as the younger man did most of the work. When the voices were directly in front of them, Jake and Naomi crept forward through the copse until they were within sight of the grave but still hidden in the trees.

The spade made a dull sound as it hit wood under the dirt. The young man bent to brush the earth from a coffin.

"Soixante-dix-sept," he said, reading a number from the tattooed wood.

"C'est ici," the older man replied with a half smile. "Bon travail, Marc."

He pulled out a smartphone and dialed a number, spoke a few words, then held the phone up to witness the find.

"Creusez," the man said. *Dig.*

Jake turned to Naomi and signaled for her to wait. Her eyes were shining, her weapon held in unwavering hands. He could see her chest rise and fall quickly, her breathing elevated. He would need to depend on her, but ideally he didn't want blood shed again today. Not here on this island of so many dead.

The younger man, Marc, shoveled the earth off the top of the coffin and stood looking down at it, his features disturbed.

"Ouvrez," the older man said, holding the phone up at an angle so the view was down into the grave.

Marc let out a torrent of French, clearly unwilling to open the coffin beneath. The older man leaned forward and cuffed him hard round the back of the head, a blow that was a promise of more. Marc raised the spade he held in a moment of rage, but stopped as he looked at the smart phone in the man's hand, his eyes darting to the older man.

After a moment, he lowered the spade and took a deep breath. He crossed himself and bent again to the coffin, levering the plywood slats from the top, breaking them open. His face contorted with disgust at his own actions.

"Regardez," Marc said, straightening, his eyes wide.

Jake held his hand up to Naomi, signaling her to be ready to move.

The older man bent forward to look into the grave, his attention fully fixed on what was below, his arm held out straight with the smart phone.

Jake burst from the bushes, his gun trained on the older man.

"Don't move," he said, his tone ice cold with quiet authority.

The two men looked up. Jake saw the older man's eyes narrow, his body twist a little as he threw the phone at Jake and reached for his gun. Jake didn't hesitate. He shot the man in the leg. The man grunted and his body spun round. Naomi stepped quickly from the trees near the wounded man, her gun held out. She kicked his weapon away, her gun trained on his head.

"Let's all just keep calm," Jake said, a little amazed that they had managed this with so little bloodshed.

Then it all went to hell.

CHAPTER 12

NAOMI STEPPED TOO CLOSE to the grave's edge, her inexperience in the field making her underestimate the young man's threat. Jake opened his mouth to shout a warning, but it was too late.

Marc spun with the spade and thrust the sharp edge into her calf, chopping into her flesh – once, twice, his face contorted with violence. She went down onto her knees with a cry. Jake reacted immediately, shooting the young man's shoulder, spinning him around. As he reared back up, spade raised for another blow, Jake shot him again in the chest. His body dropped into the grave.

The older man took advantage of the diversion and grabbed for Naomi's gun, bellowing in French, his growls those of a rabid animal. As she dodged his reach, he swung the other meaty fist, connecting with her jaw. She fell back onto the ground, collapsing with a cry as he wrestled with her for the gun.

As Jake swung his own weapon on the pair, Naomi bucked her hips and rolled into his line of fire, her back momentarily obscuring the man. Jake swore and ran closer, trying to get a better angle.

Then, a gunshot rang out and the pair were still. The metallic smell of gunfire and blood pervaded the clearing.

For a second, Jake thought Naomi must have been hit. With no field experience, she would only have fired on the range before. But then she rolled away from the older man, her face and hands and clothes splattered with gore from the close-range headshot.

Naomi clutched at her gun, her hands shaking as she held the weapon out towards the dead man as if waiting for him to rise. She moaned a little, her eyes open and staring as shock held her rigid. The wounds in her leg were bleeding, crimson jagged slices through her trouser suit and skin.

"It's OK now," Jake said, jumping quickly into the grave to check Marc's body for a pulse. The last thing they needed was retribution from the grave. But the man was dead. "You're OK now. Just breathe."

He climbed back out and went to Naomi, taking the gun from her hand and laying it beside them. He pulled her into his arms and held her shaking body.

"Sssh," he whispered, remembering his own first kill – a rebel militia gunman. It was a long time ago now, back in South Africa when he had first joined the military. There had been so many since then, but he still felt the stain of every one, even if he never knew their names. If it was death by a thousand cuts to his soul, he still had time to pay.

After a moment, Naomi wrenched her body from his, turning onto her knees beside him. She vomited, retching as she heaved up everything inside. Jake stroked her hair gently.

"I know how it feels," he said. "The first kill changes things. But your reaction means you're completely normal, believe me."

Naomi spat and wiped her mouth on her sleeve.

"They told us about this in the ARKANE academy," she said, "but we all laughed it off. You think somehow you won't ever need to fire a weapon, or to kill with one. Especially as a linguist." She exhaled and leaned her head back to look at the sky. "But I could see from his eyes that he would have finished me if he got the gun, Jake. It was him or me."

"I know, and you need to remember that if you wake in the night thinking about it." He bent to examine her leg. "Right now, you need medical attention and a tetanus shot."

"It'll be fine," Naomi said, but she flinched as he touched her.

"No, it won't be," Jake said. "Take it from me. I know about injury and this is the only body you have. We also need someone to come and deal with the dead here. What's the protocol for your office on cleanup?"

"I just have to make a call," Naomi said. "I haven't had to make this particular one before. It's a day of firsts, for sure."

"Gunshots carry across water, so chances are we'll have the Corrections Department here to arrest us in no time." He looked over at the grave. "But let's check this out first. Are you OK? Can you walk?"

Naomi nodded, rising to her feet, weight on her good leg. "I'll survive." She walked to the edge of the grave. "We need to get him out first."

Jake smiled. She was tougher than he gave her credit for.

Together they bent and grabbed the younger man under his arms, lifting the body from the grave and laying it by the side. The man had levered open the top section before they emerged from the trees, and the upper half of a skeleton lay revealed against the cheap wood. There were two things in the grave with it: a large metal cross lay around the bones of the neck, and an oilskin packet rested between its ribs – as if it had once settled on top of the body but had sunk as the corpse rotted away.

Jake stepped down carefully onto the half of the coffin that was still covered, reached down and lifted the package away from the remains. Despite the bones, the grave smelled only of earth. For a moment, Jake felt a sense of peace. This woman had died fulfilling her mission in life, helping those in true need and giving them a protection she believed worthy of them. He only hoped they could honor her memory now. He handed the package up to Naomi and climbed back out of the grave.

She unwrapped the oilskin to reveal an ivory figurine of Christ crucified, the patina similar to the Cloisters Cross they had seen this morning.

"The corpus," Naomi said. "It's beautiful." She looked up at Jake. "But should we take it from the island if she believed it would protect those here?"

"The dead don't need a relic to save them," Jake replied. "The Mother Superior brought it here for the mad, but they aren't here anymore. I think the Sisters of the Guardian Angel carry on her work, so they should have it back."

Naomi nodded and handed the figurine to him. He bent closer to look at the finely carved detail, the etching of agony on the face of the savior.

"You need to make that call now," he said. "And we need a helicopter back to Manhattan. I also think we should take the corpus back to ARKANE before we return it to the convent."

Naomi nodded and pulled a phone from her jacket pocket. She turned away as she spoke to the central ARKANE dispatch. Jake smiled at the new confidence in her voice. It had been quite a day.

He weighed the corpus in his hand as Naomi turned back, her phone call over.

"It feels heavier than I would expect for something so fragile," he said.

Naomi bent closer. "The museum exhibition suggested that some corpus icons had a cavity for a relic inside. Some piece of a saint's body, a sliver of bone, a nail from the cross or a holy thorn."

Jake turned the corpus and looked on the end of the carving, where Christ's feet were hammered together on a block. He could just make out the edges of a plug in a slightly different shade of ivory.

"Do you have a nail file, by any chance?" he asked.

"Seriously?" Naomi's look was daggers. "Just because I'm a girl, I get to carry the nail file?" Jake blushed a little and she laughed. "Actually, I do have one in my pack."

Jake jogged away and returned quickly with their two packs. Naomi pulled out a small metal nail file and Jake used it to prise the plug off. He handed it to Naomi.

"Don't lose that." He grinned. "We'll have to pretend we didn't touch it."

He looked inside and tipped the corpus, jogging it a little and shaking it gently. A small glass vial slid out wrapped in a hand-scrawled note. The paper was ivory colored and although thick, it was clearly fragile.

"Careful," Naomi whispered, but her eyes urged Jake on. He unrolled the paper and removed the vial, its dark ruby contents sticking to the sides. He read from the note.

"New Amsterdam was built on the bones of slaves but its wealth was guaranteed by the dark angel who lies bound in darkness. This blood was given for the Buttonwood men who promised to honor its release. The one who drinks must choose its fate."

"Hmmm," Naomi said. "Not particularly helpful, is it? New Amsterdam was a seventeenth-century colony on the tip of Manhattan Island, and the Dutch West Indies Company began the import of slaves to this area as laborers. I'm not sure about the rest of it."

Jake held the vial up to the fading light.

"At least we know what's in here ... but I wonder whose blood it really is."

The *whup-whup* sound of a helicopter came to them across the ocean.

"Let's get back to the open area near the asylum," Naomi said. "They can touch down there."

Jake slipped the vial and note into his pocket, plugged the

end of the now-empty corpus, and wrapped it back in the oilskin. He carefully put it in his backpack and then helped Naomi back through the trees, leaving the open grave and the bodies behind them. She limped forward, hissing a little when she stumbled and put weight on her wounded leg, but she didn't complain.

As Jake clutched the vial in his pocket, he felt a strange sensation. The world seemed to shift and he thought he saw movement in the trees. He glanced back, heart thumping, and the shadows altered. There were shades of people there, but he sensed that they weren't in this time. Perhaps not even of this place. He heard the rustle of great wings and turned quickly, expecting a figure to drop from the sky. Then the beating of helicopter blades drowned the sound out and he helped Naomi to get into the ARKANE chopper, where a medic started to dress her wounds.

As the helicopter rose into the sky, Jake looked back down at the island. Sunset tinged its contours with russet and gold, the earth absorbing the rays as it had done the blood and flesh of so many. The vial throbbed warm in his hand and Jake felt a rising need inside him, as if he was drawn to something in the city below, the feeling intensifying as they drew closer. As they swept down the edge of Manhattan Island, the sun blazed and it was as if the skyscrapers were painted in blood. Jake sensed a dark omen rise within him, something he had not felt since the crypt of the demon in Sedlec – something not of this earth.

***

Gilles Noiret slammed his fist down on the desk in front of him. The camera feed had been shut off as a tall man emerged from the trees with a gun. Gilles only got a glimpse of this man before the feed was lost.

A wracking cough shook Gilles as he screamed his frustration, and he sat back down heavily, waiting for the fit to subside, clutching a handkerchief to his mouth. When he pulled the cloth away, it was speckled with black blood. He didn't have much time, and that bastard held his last hope in the real corpus.

Once he was in control of his body again, Gilles called his team.

"I'm sending a photo of the man who now has the corpus. Find him and get me that vial."

CHAPTER 13

THE HELICOPTER LANDED AT the downtown Manhattan heliport on Pier 6 in the East River. Naomi was looking increasingly pale and the temporary dressing on her leg was sodden with blood.

"You need to get to a hospital," Jake said. "I'll take the corpus back to ARKANE myself."

She hesitated and he could see how torn she was, desperate to finish what they had started together. But after a moment she nodded, wincing as Jake helped her away from the helicopter towards a waiting car.

"The Buttonwood men," she said as they walked across the tarmac. "I was thinking about it as we flew over – anything to keep my mind off the pain. It was the Buttonwood agreement in the late eighteenth century that began the New York Stock Exchange."

The words set off a thrum within Jake, as if finally the correct chords had been struck. His whole body resonated and the vial burned in his pocket. He was overwhelmed with the need to get to the Stock Exchange building, only a few blocks away on Wall Street. He tried to control his voice, not wanting to betray the turmoil inside.

"I'll check it out," he said.

"Call me when you know anything." Naomi climbed into

the ARKANE car waiting at the curb. Jake nodded as she pulled the door shut, waving as she turned to look behind, her eyes betraying a mixture of frustration and relief.

Jake began the walk up to Wall Street, the throb of the vial in his pocket getting stronger as he strode away from the heliport towards the ferry terminal and then up Broadway. If he had been a new agent, perhaps he would have taken the vial straight to the lab, spooked by its unusual properties. But in his time at ARKANE he had seen some strange things, and curiosity now overcame doubt. After the demon in the Sedlec crypt and his days in the darkness of coma, the edges of the world had blurred and he was more willing to consider the supernatural.

He had learned that what many saw as fantasy was sometimes more real than the physical world, and truth often wore a veil. There were depths to the world that few perceived because humanity primarily trusted in the physical senses. But now that he knew there was more, Jake trusted that whatever was in the vial would lead him on. He clutched it in his hand and felt a craving, a taste in his mouth like hunger. He didn't know what for, but he felt drawn forward, north towards Wall Street.

The streets were crowded and Jake dodged the slow-moving tourists as he walked at the fast pace of native New Yorkers. As he traveled, he became aware of unusual figures on the sidewalk around him, shades of the past weaving with the present. Figures dressed in clothing from another era, vehicles that were long past vintage, and in a brief glimpse around the corner of a building, he saw ancient forest encroaching on the city streets. A realm with no people, a past too far back even for this great city. Jake experienced a sense of vertigo as he witnessed these things, his mind unsure how to process them. He pulled his hand away from the vial in his pocket and for a moment, the world was normal again. Yet he craved to touch it again, like the edges of an addiction he knew could destroy him.

Then ahead, Jake saw a face in the crowd, a man with rough features staring at him. The man's eyes narrowed as he spotted his prey, and he spoke quickly into a cell phone. Jake ducked into a side street, ran down a block and zigzagged northeast, away from the main Broadway drag.

He should have known that those who wanted the corpus would be after him. He felt for the vial in his pocket. Did they know about the blood inside? He should run for ARKANE, get in a cab, and hide in the labs beneath the UN. The technicians there could work out what was in the vial and the mystery would be solved – he could go home to London. But he felt drawn onwards, unable to resist the sensation. It was like a clock ticking down to a climax, the timer seconds away from detonation. Urgency spurred him onwards.

Jake continued north, walking swiftly, eyes forward like a local. At the back of Trinity Church, he cut along Rector Street, emerged again on Broadway and then crossed over to Wall Street and then Broad Street. Tourists lined up near the security rails to gaze up at the grand entrance to the New York Stock Exchange. He joined the back of a tour group from the Wall Street Experience as the guide launched into his spiel.

"The classical facade of the building is topped with a triangular pediment." The guide pointed up to the top of the building before them. "It may surprise you to know that the sculpted figure in the middle represents Integrity. She stretches her arms out to protect the works of man beside her – science, industry and agriculture." He gave a wry smile. "Of course, we've all lived through the financial crisis of 2008, so I'm sure you all understand what integrity means these days."

Jake tuned out the man's spiel and clutched the vial in his pocket, trying to understand what he should do next. He was drawn to this building, but there was no way of getting inside the Stock Exchange without immense security protocols. ARKANE could arrange access, but he felt sure there was no time now. These barriers were the closest he could get.

Suddenly, he felt a prickle on the back of his neck, a heightened sense of being watched. Jake turned to survey the area, picking out one, two … no, three watchers, their eyes fixed on him. They began to walk toward him, fanning out to prevent his escape in any direction. He was hemmed in.

Jake calculated the distance to the doors of the Stock Exchange building. If he jumped the barrier and ran for it, chances are he would be shot by security wary of a terrorist attack. If he waited here, these men would surround him within a minute.

He clutched the vial in his hand, feeling it pulse in time with his heartbeat. He could taste blood in his mouth. The thought electrified him.

These men didn't want the corpus.

They wanted what was inside.

Time and space are nothing for those who stand beyond. The strange words from the book of John Dee rang through his mind. Was this truly a relic that could reveal the supernatural realm? That could give a bargaining power to the one who drank.

Jake's rational mind chastised the ridiculous idea as the ravings of a man who had finally broken and should leave behind this agent life. But part of him thrilled at the thought, the audacity of faith that there might be more than this.

He looked around at the faces of the tourists who had come to worship at the temple of Mammon, their disapproval of what went on in these hallowed halls hiding a desire to be just like those within. Behind them he could see more figures, as the moment flicked in and out of history before his eyes. Above the hubbub of the street, he thought he could hear the beat of giant wings.

The men stepped closer, hands in their jacket pockets, clearly concealing weapons. Jake had seconds before they were on him.

He pulled the vial from his pocket and took the stopper from the lid. Jake had expected the metallic scent of blood, but all he could smell was the chill stone of a cave beneath the earth.

His heart beat faster, a hammering in his chest as he approached a fulcrum of time, a tipping point that would take him into the unknown. He was sure of one thing – this blood, whatever it was, could not fall into the hands of these Confessors.

But what would drinking it do to him?

Jake felt reckless in that moment. He remembered lying in a coma, the warmth of a black blanket over his mind, a detachment from the world. He was no longer afraid of dying – in truth, part of him longed for the end of it all.

As the men closed in around him, the vial pulsed in his hand. Jake lifted it to his lips, tipping his head back to gulp the warm liquid, his throat burning as it went down.

CHAPTER 14

THE LIQUID SEEMED TO set his body on fire and for a moment, Jake thought he would be consumed by an inner flame.

Then the world shifted and shimmered. The people around him faded and the noise of the world dulled. It was as if he stepped through a waterfall into a world beyond, into the cave he had smelled in the vial.

No, not a cave. It was a crypt, somewhere hewn deep in the rock under Manhattan. And in the darkness, he could feel ... something.

Jake heard the whisper of wings and the flutter of breath before he saw it.

The chamber was vast and dark, his footsteps a faint echo as he walked towards the sound. As his eyes adjusted to the dark, he realized that the whole place was crisscrossed with shining lines, ropes of spun silver and precious metal that held the captive in place and gave the place an eerie light.

An angel, if that's what it was, hung suspended in the center of the crypt, its pale skin hooked through with barbs, its arms outstretched and pulled apart by the shining cords in a parody of crucifixion. Its shape was as a man, its torso rippled with muscle, with a loincloth of sorts wrapped around its slim hips. There was a sheen to its skin, a translucence like alabaster. Its wings looked to be over six feet in length, densely feathered and beautiful, but they were pinioned to its body by loops of silver chain.

The angel lifted its head, its perfect features set in an expression of sorrow. Jake met its dark eyes and fell to his knees as vertigo shot through him, a sense of shifting in time and space to a place apart, somehow separate – as if the world had begun to spin around this underground prison.

Its eyes were the green of the depths of the ocean and the sparkle of a thousand stars, and it saw right through him. Jake wanted to look away but the angel wouldn't shift its gaze, studying him as a man might study a nest of ants before he burns it down, uncaring of mass slaughter. Jake sensed the angel scanning his memory, reading his past, noting the scars on his body and his psyche. He felt violated in that moment and yet, when it relaxed its gaze, the emptiness was a kind of freedom.

It has been long years since men came here. It is past time you released me.

Jake heard the words in his head but nothing was said aloud. The angel spoke directly into his mind.

I know you, Jake Timber. I see your past. Release me and I will give you what you desire most.

Images of his murdered family surfaced in Jake's mind, his father and mother holding out their hands to him, smiling as they welcomed him home. His youngest sister, lying in the porch swing, reading a book, her young body no longer broken and violated. The house at Walkerville was bright, lit by the sun. There was no blood on the walls, no stink of rotten, flyblown flesh in the air.

"You can bring them back?" Jake said in wonder, wanting to hold onto the glimpses of a life he had lost.

I can take you back and you can stop it. Kill before they do.

Jake saw the faces of the gang who had carried out the atrocity, each one a hated countenance. He had hunted them down afterwards and killed them, revenging his family before fleeing the country. But the grief was with him every day.

If he could go back, he could be at home the day before the gang came. He would be ready for them and his sisters, his parents, would still be alive. Tears welled up within him and he gulped them back. For so many years, he had lived with the guilt of their deaths. Was this the answer?

The angel's face flinched suddenly, as if it was being forced to speak further by some unseen power.

I can give you the peace you seek. I can bring your family to life again. But I – must – also show you what will happen to this city if you release me.

Jake's mind was filled with flame and he reeled back at the stink of smoke. The haze cleared, and he looked out at Manhattan Island as if he was back in the helicopter, looking down as it swooped over the city.

The downtown area was now a mass of burning buildings, the screams of people below a cacophony of pain and death. There were riots on the streets and the police were overwhelmed by brutality, driven back by hordes of rampaging men. People plunged into the waters around the island to escape the violence, only to be consumed by dark shapes that dragged them under, leaving dark patches of blood on the surface as their bodies were ripped apart. Creatures leapt across the chasms between buildings, dragging bodies for feasting and violation. It was a scene of Hell from a Hieronymus Bosch painting, something that could only spring from the mind of madness. Jake tried to shut out the sight but the images were forced into his head, a tableau of slaughter.

I am a hostage for the city, a shield against its destruction, for while I am here, this island cannot fall to the dark powers. But if I am released, then vengeance will fall for its years of corruption.

The images faded and Jake breathed deeply, inhaling the

cold of the crypt, his mind whirling at all he had seen. He pointed at the ties that bound the angel.

"You don't look like a willing hostage."

The angel's face twisted, hate rippling over its features.

I was hung here to pay for my own sins.

"What did you do?" Jake asked.

You might have called it love.

The angel's voice in his head was faint as Jake had a vision of a beautiful woman, laughing as she splashed in a stream, her naked body dripping and glistening in the sun. Jake felt the angel's lust for her, but there was something beneath it, a jealousy and a need to possess that which he could never attain himself. As the woman turned, he saw that she was pregnant, her breasts full and heavy. She giggled as the angel stroked her with its wings but the sense of transgression of natural law weighed heavily upon the scene.

"Nephilim," Jake whispered and the vision dissolved.

The angel bowed its head.

For my sins, I am bound here. Only after seventy times seventy years will I be released from this earthly prison by He who imprisoned me here. But your kind are curious, Jake Timber.

The early men of New York found this place, and promised me release if I helped them establish the city, giving them insight and knowledge that would bestow wealth and power upon them. They promised to free me when they had achieved their goals – I gave them my blood so they would return. Ever since, I have awaited that day. Now you are here.

"Those men are long dead," Jake said. He closed his eyes for a moment and took a deep breath. "And I cannot release you if it means the city will fall under some dark destruction. There is already much suffering above, but there are people who bring light."

Jake thought of Naomi and her desire to help the people of the city. Regina and the Sisters of the Guardian Angel.

His time with ARKANE and how he would never have been recruited by Marietti if he hadn't fled South Africa in the aftermath of his family's tragedy. He thought of Morgan.

"As much as I want my family back," he said. "That time is passed. I cannot take your exchange, even for them."

Time is nothing.

The angel's features twisted in anguish.

"Then your many years in chains should pass quickly," Jake said in a soft voice.

Then you must return above. I will let you go if you take another vial of my blood. For then another can make a choice as you have done, for the next generation.

Jake hesitated, knowing that others would choose differently – that to take the vial back up would put the city under threat.

You have no choice if you want to return to your life. Approach and bring the vial.

Jake stepped through the maze of silver cords, twisting and turning to avoid touching them. As he drew closer, he could see the muscle tone under its skin, a deeply masculine beauty of sculpted marble. This angel was a warrior and surely no man could stand against it, or others like it, if it was free.

Yes, there are more of my kind, but we are not so concerned with your lives. Don't worry, Jake Timber. You have enough of your own troubles ahead.

Jake inched closer until he was standing directly before the angel, looking up into its terrible beauty.

"You see my future?"

Of course, time is nothing. Release me and I will tell you. Use the knife below and cut the ties that bind me.

Its green eyes burned like a fire of emerald and for a moment, Jake was hypnotized by their promise. He bent and picked up the silver knife that lay on the ground beneath the angel. Its handle was bright, reflecting the light from the cords and the glow of the angel's body.

He shook his head, breaking the gaze.

"I'm sorry. I can't."

The angel nodded.

Then use the knife and catch my blood in the vial. Then I will release you.

Jake held the vial up and used the knife to cut into the angel's side, where the lance that pierced Christ would have slipped in. Blood welled from the wound and Jake caught the first few drops in the vial before stoppering the lid once more. As he watched, the cut closed and the angel's skin was whole and unblemished again.

There was a pitcher with water on the floor next to a wooden drinking cup. A simple torture, since it would be forever out of the angel's reach. Jake poured some water out and lifted it to the angel's lips. Its green eyes softened and for a second, he saw a glimpse of the beyond in its gaze. A stab of hope rose within Jake as the angel drank deeply until the cup was drained.

Thank you.

Jake heard a rushing sound fill the crypt and the angel faded into a shimmering silver mist. He dropped the cup and clutched at his ears, trying to equalize the pressure by gulping. As the mist cleared, he found himself back in front of the New York Stock Exchange, the moment frozen as he had left it.

But there was something different in his body. He sensed the change. There was no throb of pain from his old injuries, no hesitation in his muscle memory. He felt revived. Had the angel's blood healed him?

Time began again, but slowly at first. He slipped past one of the men who came for him and walked away as time sped up and life resumed. From a safe distance, Jake looked back to see the men milling about in confusion as they searched for him and he ducked into a side street heading back to

ARKANE. The vial of angel's blood in his pocket was cold now, with no sense of power. The corpus would go back to the nuns, but this would go down into the ARKANE vaults away from those who might be tempted to use it.

CHAPTER 15

JAKE STOOD ON THE back of the Staten Island commuter ferry watching the sunset turn the sky orange behind the Statue of Liberty. He had wanted to see this view before he left New York, and knew he had enough time before his evening flight home. Naomi was recovering in hospital and was enthusiastic about turning her skills to being a field agent. The Cloisters Cross had been recovered from the penthouse flat of reclusive billionaire Gilles Noiret, who had been found dead, his body rotted by poison. The Sisters of the Guardian Angel had chosen to give the corpus to the museum to be displayed on the shaft of the cross. It had been a big day, and for once Jake thought that his sleep might be without nightmares.

Wisps of cloud painted the horizon with shades of pink and burnt umber and he remembered the visions of the angel, the glimpse into a realm that seemed just a hallucination now. Jake took a deep breath, inhaling the ocean air, his lungs expanding. His body definitely felt stronger now, and there was no pain from the wounds he had suffered over the last ARKANE missions. He would need to get scans to confirm it when he got home, but he was sure the angel's blood had healed him.

But there was something more.

The cracks in his mind, the guilt over his murdered family – they were still there but they were softer now, as if the edges had been rubbed off. The scars were no longer raw and angry, but part of his body. He would always be aware of them, but they didn't own him anymore. Had the angel given him this gift after a moment of compassion in the crypt? He would never know.

Jake wondered how much of the day's events to write in his official report, and what he would label the vial for the ARKANE crypt. What would he tell Morgan? Maybe nothing. Maybe only that he was able to recover the relic and return it to the convent, that the Cloisters Cross had been retrieved, that the vial needed to be kept safe.

He smiled and looked back at the famous skyline. New York had its problems but it was a vibrant city that would survive another generation, unknowing of what lay chained beneath.

The ferry horn honked. A lone seagull rode the wind on the wake of the boat and as he gazed into the froth of the water, Jake knew his future was with ARKANE. He was strong again now and once he flew home, he would be back on duty alongside Morgan, as the partner she deserved.

AUTHOR'S NOTE

AS EVER, MY BOOKS are based on real historical places with truth twisted into fiction and this one is no different! You can see the visual inspiration for the book at: www.pinterest.com/jfpenn/new-york/

New York

It's difficult to write about New York without resorting to cliché movie locations, but in the Cloisters, I found a little slice of medieval England.

The chapters about the Cloisters are based on *The Cloisters Cross: Its Art and Meaning*, and *A Walk through the Cloisters*. Both publications are available from the Met in free PDF format here:

http://www.metmuseum.org/visit/visit-the-cloisters

The Cloisters Cross is as described except for the Enochian script, which is actually considered to be Hebrew written backwards.

I've walked the fantastic High Line in Manhattan and I highly recommend it to anyone wanting a little escape from the New York city streets. There is a church of the Guardian Angel in Manhattan, but everything about the nuns is fictionalized.

The scene in the subway tunnels was based on the video of *Undercity* featuring urban historian Steve Duncan. You can watch it here: www.vimeo.com/18280328

Also, check out www.undercity.org for more underground adventures.

You can find out about the vaults under the New York Public Library here:

http://gothamist.com/2008/10/24/underneath_the_new_york_public_libr.php#photo-1

Hart Island is indeed a mass burial ground, and I have tried to honor the location, although I haven't been there. There was an asylum and they did manufacture shoes.

www.untappedcities.com/2013/07/22/abandoned-hart-island-new-york-citys-mass-burial-ground/

Angels

The idea for the angel chained under the city came from a sculpture I saw while walking in London – an angel's wing rising from the streets near the Bank of England. I had a vision of this huge supernatural being trapped under the heavy buildings. Then I saw the bound fallen angel by Paul Fryer in his art installation Morning Star, and the two ideas fused in this book.

Thanks for joining Morgan and the ARKANE team!

If you loved the book and have a moment to spare, I would really appreciate a short review where you bought the book. Your help in spreading the word is gratefully appreciated.

You can also get a free copy of the bestselling ARKANE thriller, *Day of the Vikings*, when you sign up to join my Reader's Group at:

WWW.JFPENN.COM/FREEBOOK

More books in the international bestselling ARKANE thriller series. Described by readers as 'Dan Brown meets Lara Croft.'
Available in print, ebook and audio formats at all online stores.

Stone of Fire #1
Crypt of Bone #2
Ark of Blood #3
One Day in Budapest #4
Day of the Vikings #5
Gates of Hell #6
One Day in New York #7

The London Psychic Series. Described by readers as 'the love child of Stephen King and PD James.'
Available in ebook, print and audio formats.

Desecration
Delirium
Deviance

A Thousand Fiendish Angels, short stories inspired by Dante's Inferno, on the edge of thriller and the occult

WWW.JFPENN.COM

ABOUT J.F.PENN

JOANNA PENN IS THE *New York Times* and *USA Today* bestselling author of thrillers on the edge. Joanna has a Master's degree in Theology from the University of Oxford, Mansfield College and a Graduate Diploma in Psychology from the University of Auckland, New Zealand.

She lives in London, England but spent eleven years in Australia and New Zealand. Joanna worked for thirteen years as an international business consultant within the IT industry, but is now a full-time author-entrepreneur. She is the author of the ARKANE series as well as other thrillers, crime and horror.

Joanna is a PADI Divemaster and enjoys traveling as often as possible. She is obsessed with religion and psychology and loves to read, drink Pinot Noir and soak up European culture through art, architecture and food.

You can sign up for Joanna's newsletter, with giveaways and the latest releases, here:
www.JFPenn.com/list

Connect with Joanna online:

(e) joanna@JFPenn.com

(w) www.JFPenn.com

(t) @thecreativepenn

(f) www.facebook.com/JFPennAuthor

www.pinterest.com/jfpenn/

Joanna Penn also writes non-fiction. Available in print and ebook formats.

Career Change: Stop hating your job,
discover what you really want to do, and start doing it!

How To Market A Book

Public Speaking For Authors,
Creatives and Other Introverts

Business for Authors: How to be an Author Entrepreneur

For writers:

Joanna's site www.TheCreativePenn.com helps people write, publish and market their books through articles, audio, video and online products as well as live workshops. Joanna is available internationally for speaking events aimed at writers, authors and entrepreneurs. Joanna also has a popular podcast for writers on iTunes, The Creative Penn.

ACKNOWLEDGEMENTS

THANKS, AS EVER, TO my great team of professionals: Jen Blood at Adian Editing for the fantastic editing, Derek Murphy at Creativindie for cover design, Wendy Janes at WendyProof.co.uk for proofreading and Jane Dixon Smith at JDSmith-Design.com for the print formatting.

Thanks to my readers and especially to my PennFriends. Your continued support allows me to write these stories, which makes me a happy writer and, hopefully, makes you a happy reader!